CLAUDIA ON

Claudia on the Wing

RAINBOW
ROMANCE

STELLA KENT

ROBERT HALE · LONDON

© Stella Kent 1994
First published in Great Britain 1994

ISBN 0 7090 5509 9

Robert Hale Limited
Clerkenwell House
Clerkenwell Green
London EC1R 0HT

Photoset in North Wales by
Derek Doyle & Associates, Mold, Clwyd.
Printed and bound by Interprint Limited,
Valletta, Malta.

One

Thank heaven Jenny's plea had come by post, Claudia thought. If she had telephoned, what might I have blurted out? Something stupid. Something revealing.

She pulled the letter from its envelope to re-read its conclusion '... *I know it's a lot to ask when we haven't been close for a long time, but I've no one else to turn to. Please say you'll help, if only for a little while until I can arrange something else. The children would love to see you, and Peter, too....*'

Claudia put down the letter and poured herself a cup of coffee. '*We haven't been close for a long time.*' The nearest sweet-natured Jenny would ever come to a reproof, for it was Claudia who had been responsible for the breach. But not without good reason. She wrenched the closing words from their context as eagerly as a lovesick schoolgirl. '*...the children would love to see you, and Peter, too....*' As she re-read the words the old longing swept over her, her feeling for Peter and his for her that made it impossible for her to see her dearest friend.

At one time their phone calls had been constant, an uninhibited outpouring of news, gossip, secrets. But once Peter filled her heart, how could she bear to hear the details of his family life? Their calls had

5

grown stilted and less frequent until birthday and
Christmas cards were the only contact. It had been
painful, not least Jenny's pained bewilderment.
Perhaps she had thought that Claudia, with her
more exciting lifestyle, found her own situation
boring. Claudia smiled wryly, remembering how
often she had longed to trade places.

She picked up her cup and sipped the cooling
coffee. The toast in its rack had long since gone
cold. The letter had dropped on to the doormat
just as she had sat down to breakfast and, at the
sight of Jenny's handwriting, all thoughts of eating
had left her.

What was she to do? Her first thought had been
that Jenny was going to be passing through the city
and wanted to meet. She could have dealt with that,
been out of town on an assignment. She had done
it before. But this was no proposal to catch up on
gossip with an old friend, this was a cry from the
heart. And, if she knew Jenny, it was an
understated cry. She would never have made it
unless she was in desperate straits. Moreover it was
a plea that Claudia could answer. Her work-time
was flexible and she had little scheduled in the next
month.

She put down her cup purposefully. There were
more important things than her own tender
feeling. It was time to grow up. She cleared the
breakfast dishes, carrying them through to the
kitchen. She would need to phone her mother to
arrange to have her post collected and urgent
messages redirected. Then she must phone Jenny
and discuss her plans.

She glanced at the clock. It was 8.15. Her mother
wouldn't yet have left for the school where she was

deputy headmistress. She dropped on to the settee and pulled the phone towards her.

Her mother would be delighted that she was re-establishing contact with Jenny. Jenny, with her artless milkmaid prettiness, incapable of guile, was exactly the sort of friend of whom mothers approved. And Jenny, orphaned as a child and deposited with unloving grandparents, had returned the affection. The rift had upset Claudia's mother, as had Claudia's refusal to discuss it, but she had been wise enough to leave the subject alone.

Claudia dialled and, in a moment, heard her mother's clear, warm voice. 'Claudia? This is an early call. I only have a few minutes, darling.'

'I know, Mum. I just wanted to ask you to pick up my mail and get the messages off the machine for a few days.'

'Of course I will. When are you leaving?'

'I don't know yet. I'll give you the details when I do. I just wanted to clear it with you.'

'You know it's no trouble. I practically pass the end of your street. Will you be gone long?'

'I don't know that either.'

'Very mysterious—'

Claudia recognized the unspoken, *Have you met someone?* and smiled. 'It is. I've had a letter from Jenny.'

'Jenny Liddell? I thought you had lost touch with her.'

'Not completely, but this was a bolt from the blue. She seems to be in some sort of trouble and wants me to help out.'

'To go and stay with them?' Claudia caught a doubtful note in her mother's expressive voice.

'Apparently.'

'They're not still living in Durham, are they?'

'No, the address is somewhere in the wilds of Northumberland. Goodness knows what they're doing there. I'm going to phone Jenny when we've rung off. I expect to get the details then.'

'She has two children, hasn't she?'

'Yes. Amy and Ben. They'll be about three and four now.'

'Well, let me know when you want me to start and where to forward any messages. Give my love to Jenny and tell her if there's anything I can do to help....'

'Thanks, Mum. I'll tell her. I'll let you get off now. I'll ring again later.'

Claudia put down the phone. Her mother hadn't mentioned Peter. With her ultra-sensitive antennae she never did, but she would be concerned about the situation.

She decided to wait a few moments before phoning Jenny. Probably mothers of young children were busy at this hour. Perhaps Peter wouldn't have left for work and would pick up the phone.... She frowned in irritation. If she was still in that idiotic frame of mind what hope did she have of getting through this visit unscathed?

She looked around her living-room with pleasure and pride. A shaft of early spring sunshine made a golden path across the polished wood floor. It was a spacious room stretching across the whole first floor of the old terraced house. There was a fine plasterwork frieze and cornice. Two high sash windows were framed in glazed cotton. At one end a circular beech table and chairs formed a dining area. The larger lounging area held a comfortable

sofa and easy chairs, small tables and an antique
walnut bureau. Silken rugs adorned the floor.
There was a wall of books and the latest in hi-fi,
video and TV.

Beyond the living-room was a luxuriously
appointed bathroom, a smart kitchen and a small
second bedroom that Claudia had turned into an
office-cum-studio where she worked at her arts and
crafts and occasional journalism. Everything was
tasteful and carefully chosen and most of it was
expensive. It had not been easily come by. She had
worked and saved hard for her treasured pos-
sessions.

She went into the kitchen and washed her few
dishes, then to the bedroom where she pulled out an
overnight bag and a small suitcase before she
acknowledged that she was playing for time. She
had no idea of what was to be asked of her. She
returned to the living-room where she sat down and
dialled the number on Jenny's letter.

As the phone rang Claudia became aware that she
was clutching the receiver painfully tight. Then
Jenny's voice replied, unmistakable, but with a
wariness in it that Claudia had never heard before.

She said, 'Jenny? I've just got your letter....'

'I feel terrible writing to you in that way, but I
couldn't think of anything else to do.'

'But what's the matter? You know I'll help if I can.'

'Oh, Claudia!' Jenny's voice was rough, as though
she was fighting back tears. 'It's great to hear your
voice.'

'It's wonderful to hear from you. I'm sorry it's
been so long.'

'I understand. I know you must be busy. But – are
you free for a little while?'

'Right now?'

'Well, as soon as possible.'

'I haven't much on in the next couple of weeks. I take it I could work on a couple of jobs while I was with you? Just magazine articles.'

'Of course. That's why I thought of you – that being freelance you might be able to get away. And, anyway, there just wasn't anybody else.'

'Gee, thanks!'

'I didn't mean it like that. I'd sooner have you than anybody in the world. It just seemed such a nerve to ask. Peter was furious when I suggested it.'

Once again Claudia was conscious of her hand clenched on the receiver. 'Was he?'

'Livid. He couldn't bear you to know we were in trouble. You know Peter, it's just his pride.'

'How does he feel now? I wouldn't want to come if it would embarrass him.'

'I made him see that there was no alternative. But he insisted that if I sensed any reluctance on your part I was to back off.' Jenny gave the little gurgle of laughter that Claudia remembered so well. 'I thought I could safely promise that. You know me, I never pick up nuances.'

No, Claudia thought with some pride, you never did. Even when our hearts were breaking we never gave you the slightest hint.

She said lightly, 'But what is it you want me to do, for heaven's sake? I'm keeping my reluctance on hold, just in case.'

Jenny sobered. 'It seems a lot to ask, but could you come and stay for a few days? I don't mean to do the housework, Peter can manage that, but just to fill the gaps. I'll do my best to get someone to take over after that, although the place is so far off the beaten track that it won't be easy.'

'But Jenny, what's the matter? Are you ill?'

'Not exactly. The fact is I'm pregnant again and, instead of the easy romp that the last two were, things have been going wrong. If I'm not to lose the baby I have to rest up, maybe have a couple of days in hospital.'

'I'm so sorry. I'll certainly come and I have no hang-ups whatever about housework. It will be a welcome change from tiptoeing around some of the prima-donna egos I have to deal with.'

'Thanks, Claudia. I knew I could count on you. The standard of housekeeping isn't very high, anyway, with my two little demons around, so a slight deterioration won't be noticed. If, for instance, you could ferry them to their nursery school it would be a great help.'

'Of course, no problem. But will they be happy to stay with me? They were only tiny the last time I saw them.'

'Oh, Peter will be around most of the time, even if I am whisked away.'

'But won't he be at work? It isn't the school holiday, is it?'

There was a brief pause and when Jenny spoke again some of the pleasure had gone from her voice. 'Peter isn't teaching anymore.'

'He isn't?' Claudia was surprised. Peter had stepped into a job, teaching a Poly foundation course, almost straight from art school and, the last Claudia had heard, had been relishing it. 'What is he doing? For that matter, what are you doing in the back-of-beyond?'

'We artists can exist anywhere, you know, Claudia.' Jenny's attempt at humour didn't quite ring true. 'There's a lot to tell, but I don't want to talk over the phone. Things haven't been going well.'

'We'll talk when I'm with you. And I can certainly take this present emergency off your shoulders.'

'Just talk will be wonderful.' There was no mistaking the tears in Jenny's voice now. 'When can you get here?'

'Today, if you like. I have to clear up a few loose ends. I can be with you by late afternoon.'

'That's great. The road is quite straighforward. After Newcastle you take the A696 to Otterburn. About four miles past Otterburn turn left into a minor road signposted Marling. It's a small village and the turn for Brackenfield is just before it. I'll get Peter to wait at the end of the lane for you.'

'That won't be necessary.'

'Don't you believe it! People get over-confident on the last stage and wander around lost for hours. So – I'll see you then?'

'Yes. Goodbye, Jenny.'

Claudia replaced the receiver, her emotions in a turmoil. She was not only to live under the same roof as Peter, but, possibly, with Jenny absent. How could she go through with it? She caught herself snatching at Jenny's words. 'Things haven't been going well.' Did she mean between herself and Peter? That was often the meaning of the phrase. She shuddered with self-disgust. Jenny was pregnant. Surely that meant all was well with their relationship.

She got to her feet and returned to the kitchen where she made some fresh coffee. There were practical things to be done. Packing and sorting out some work. Phone calls to cancel engagements and instructions to leave on her mother's answering machine. A call on her downstairs neighbours to inform them of her absence. It might be helpful if she took some provisions to Jenny's, gifts for the children....

She drank her coffee looking out of the window over the rooftops. Why, she wondered, had Peter given up teaching after so brief a period? Some of their art-school friends had dreamed of opting out of the rat-race and making a living from their skills. Throwing pots and weaving garments in some remote picturesque cottage. Perhaps taking their wares around the county fairs.

It would be a hard option with four – soon five – mouths to feed and anyway, neither Peter or Jenny had been drawn to that kind of homespun scenario. They had both had a wide range of interests. Peter had been enthusiastic over his Poly post and, although Jenny had started her family soon after graduation, she, too, had been keen to teach when the children were older. But people change and perhaps they had thought it would benefit the children to be brought up away from the city.

She rinsed her cup and went into the bedroom where she considered what to pack. The country-side in early March suggested warm and casual. The place would probably be bleak after her comfortable flat. She decided on two pairs of trousers, two skirts and a variety of sweaters, then added underwear, pyjamas and warm tights to her case. Absolutely nothing glamorous, she thought wryly. This is an old family friend come to look after the children.

In the bathroom, collecting her toilet requisites, she passed the mirror glimpsing her face startlingly pale. She turned to regard herself fully. Would Jenny – and Peter – find her changed? Three years was a long time and she had grown away from the impetuous art student of those days. Her tawny hair and green-hazel eyes beneath winging brows, her wide mouth, still hinted at passion, but it was overlaid now with control and reserve. She turned away shrugging, then changed into a cornflower-blue sweater and navy cord trousers for the journey, adding her robe to the suitcase.

She went into the smaller bedroom which she had arranged as a workroom where she pursued the different activities that made up her career. Against one wall stood a desk with a typewriter and a small computer, opposite it a bank of filing cabinets. In the centre of the room stood a large table beneath strip-lighting. On the table were paints and enamels, jewellery-making equipment and swatches of brilliant silk for her current commission – a range of scarves for a select boutique. Claudia's success lay in having several strings to her bow. She designed and made jewellery and small accessories, her delicate watercolours and exquisite needlework were in great demand. She contributed articles to craft magazines and glossy monthlies and had a regular column in a regional newspaper highlighting craftspeople, shows and exhibitions in the area. It was a very satisfying life with a good financial return and the freedom to work at her own inclination.

She hurried around, tidying and locking cupboards. It was probably impractical to take work with her, so she collected the rough notes for her latest article and a fat paperback she had long intended to read. She made a few professional calls before composing a message for her mother's machine giving Jenny's address and phone number and a brief outline of the situation.

She slipped on her navy reefer jacket, picked up her bag and ran downstairs. She hesitated outside the door to the ground-floor flat. The Werners, her Viennese-born neighbours, were kind and charming, but inclined to be garrulous. However, they would have to be told if the flat was empty.

As she raised her hand to the bell Paul Werner came puffing up the steps to the front door, a newspaper in his hand. His face broke into a delighted smile. 'Ah, Claudia, you will come in and have some coffee? Maria will be so pleased.'

'Thank you, Paul, but I really can't stop. I just wanted to tell you that I have to go away for a few days – something has come up suddenly. My mother will be calling in for my mail.'

'I shall look out for her. But are you well, Claudia? To me you look pale. Always so busy, hurry, scurry!'

Claudia smiled. 'I'm fine, Paul. But I must scurry now. Give my love to Maria.'

She turned away, leaving the old man hatching plans to waylay her mother, and ran down the steps. Her car was at the kerb and she slid behind the wheel. There was a group of shops less than half-a-mile away, so she had no need to drive into the city. Once there, she withdrew some cash. In the small supermarket she selected half-a-dozen ready-to-eat meals, a large fruitcake and some fresh fruit. There was little choice of anything to take for the children, but, in the bookshop, she was delighted to find an *Orlando* book and a well-illustrated alphabet book. As an afterthought she added a roadmap of Northumbria.

When she returned to her flat it was almost noon and she studied her map over coffee and a sandwich. Marling was not to be found but, although Otterburn was farther north than she had realized – not far from the Scottish border – once she was past Newcastle the road was straightforward.

When she had finished her lunch she tucked the map into her handbag, locked up the flat and carried her case down to the car.

She took the road north out of the city, seeing to her left the magnificent bulk of Durham Cathedral outlined against the pale-blue sky. The road to Newcastle was familiar, but busy enough for her to need to concentrate on her driving. Winding her way through the city and out on to the Jedburgh road likewise required her full attention.

When the last outskirts of the city fell behind her she began, once more, to consider what lay ahead of her. She was determined not to give Peter the slightest hint of how she felt about him. And would she still feel the same way about him? Surely Peter, with his family and a new baby expected, would have put his feelings for her behind him? He was an honourable man, he had made his decision and stuck to it. How wonderful it would be, she thought wistfully, if they could return to the way they once had been, three loving friends together.

As she sped north along the open road Peter and Jenny's decision to settle in these parts became easier to understand. She had forgotten the sublime beauty of this lonely landscape, the gently folding hills, the heather moors and, ahead of her, the looming Cheviots and the dark forests of Redesdale and Kielder. But how were they supporting themselves? There seemed to be nothing except sheep farming. If they were trying to make a living from craftwork, perhaps she would be able to help with publicity and contacts. Both Jenny and Peter had been tatented artists.

Such conjectures kept her mind occupied until she suddenly saw the signpost for Otterburn. Her foot touched the brake, her nerves jangling. She was almost there. Past Otterburn, she soon came to a minor road posted Marling and turned into it. It was a narrow road with scarcely room for two vehicles to pass. She had travelled about two miles when she saw a red car tucked close in to the hedge. As she hesitated a man got out and raised a hand. It was Peter.

Claudia drew in behind the car, stopped and put on the handbrake. She wound down the window as Peter walked towards her. The same curling brown hair, the same expressive grey eyes, the same sweet mouth. A little older, a little more serious. She said, 'Have you been waiting long?' and, simultaneously, he said, 'This is very good of you.' They both laughed in embarrassment. Claudia tried to start again, but no words would come. Peter bent down, put an arm through the open window and cupped her face gently in his hand. He kissed her softly on the mouth. 'Claudia,' he said.

Two

A longing to return his kiss flooded through her, but she drew back. 'How are you, Peter?'

'Fine. I'm fine. You look terrific.'

'Thank you. How is Jenny?'

'She's OK as long as she rests. This really is good of you, Claudia.'

'Nonsense. I'm looking forward to seeing you all.'

'It won't interfere with your work? You seem to have a full workload. Jen and I often see your byline in the paper – and your designs in the chic outlets – when we emerge into civilization.'

Claudia laughed. 'It's not as exhausting as it sounds, as long as you're organized. Once the designs are despatched they can look after themselves.'

'You were always single-minded.'

'So, where do we go from here? Is this Brackenfield?'

'Brackenfield is the big house. We have what's called the Lower Cottage. There are two others, but they're derelict.'

'Lead on, then, and I'll follow behind.'

Peter looked at her as though there was more he wanted to say, but he turned and walked back to his

car. Getting in, he negotiated the corner into a
lane.

Claudia switched on the engine, let out the
handbrake and drew a shaky breath as she
prepared to follow him. That wasn't too bad, my
girl, she told herself. In fact you acquitted yourself
like a proper grown-up person. Just be sure to
keep it up.

A tall hedge bordered the lane above which she
could see a hillside dotted with clusters of trees.
Suddenly she saw a large stone house, plain and
square, among the trees. Peter's brake lights came
on and he turned between half-hidden gateposts.
So this was Brackenfield.

Claudia turned after him. Instead of taking the
drive that led up to the house, Peter took a track
that ran parallel to the lane they had been on. The
track rose gently until they reached a field gate.
Peter got out and propped it open and Claudia
passed through. He closed the gate and returned
to his car. After a short distance they came to a
second gate, this one standing open. Peter pulled
up alongside it, got out and locked his car. Claudia
parked beside him and got out, taking her suitcase
from the boot.

Peter took the case from her. 'Sorry about your
springs. The rains have washed the surface off the
track.' He led the way through the gate. 'Well, here
we are.'

The lane on this side of the gate widened, to
stop, fifty yards ahead, outside the cottage.

Claudia just had time to register that the cottage
was both larger and more attractive than she had
expected when the front door opened and Jenny
appeared. She wore jeans and a man's blue shirt

that concealed her pregnancy. Her fair hair was fixed up in a sort of topknot. A dark-haired little girl and a small, sturdy blond boy peeped from behind her.

A lump constricted Claudia's throat. She flew along the lane and threw her arms around her friend. 'Jenny, it's wonderful to see you!'

Jenny hugged her back, sniffing happily. 'Oh, Claudia, it's *great* to see you! I knew you'd come!'

Claudia bent down. 'And you are Amy and Ben. I knew you when you were babies, but you won't remember me.'

The children edged forward for a hug and Claudia looked up at Jenny again. 'But, Jenny, you look fine.'

'I know. You must think I'm a fraud. You think I just pulled this to lure you here.'

'Of course I don't! I'm only happy to see you looking so well.'

'I feel disgustingly well. I just have to keep my feet up. It's only five months, you see, so if anything did go wrong—'

'So why are you bouncing about?' Peter was smiling at them. 'Let's get you settled.'

'The cottage is lovely.' Claudia stepped back for a better view. The stone-built dwelling was old, but well maintained, recently re-roofed and freshly painted. 'And I imagined you starving in a garret!'

'If we lose this place we will be starving in a garret.'

Claudia looked at Peter. The smile had gone from his face. 'Is that a possibility?'

Jenny said quickly, 'Don't let's talk about that now. Peter, take Claudia's bag to her room and we'll have some tea.'

She led the way into a small hall and thence into a big living-room, pleasantly furnished with comfortable, slightly shabby furniture.

'Sorry about the mess. Peter has been doing his best, but he can't neglect his job.'

'What work does he do?'

'He works on the Brackenfield estate.'

'Do you rent the cottage?'

'No, it's a tied cottage. It goes with the job.'

And goes if the job goes? Was that one of Jenny's problems, Claudia wondered. She said, 'Let me get the tea.'

'Oh, I'm not helpless. It's only a cup for us while the children have theirs. Sit down if you can find a space. I'll officially retire tomorrow.'

Claudia handed over the food she had brought which Jenny received with no sign of embarrassment. She bore it off the kitchen while Claudia moved a selection of toys from the settee and sat down.

After a moment Peter came back downstairs. 'Your room is on the right at the top of the stairs. The bathroom is next door to it and there's a second loo down here by the back door.'

'I think I'll take advantage of that now. Will you show me the way, Amy?'

Amy eagerly took Claudia's hand and they went through the large well-equipped kitchen where Jenny was arranging plates on a tray.

Washing her hands in the lavatory, Claudia looked out of the small window at a vegetable garden and a paved patio area near the house. Beyond the house at the bottom of the garden was a broad swift-flowing stream and, beyond that, sheep grazed on a steep hillside.

She emerged to find Amy helping Jenny to carry the tea through to the living-room. There, Peter supervised the children's meal while Jenny and Claudia drank tea and ate home-made fruitcake.

When tea was finished Claudia went up to her room to unpack and to fetch the books she had brought for the children. Her bedroom was charmingly furnished and a radiator gave out a comforting warmth. A peep into the adjoining bathroom revealed a new suite with a shower cubicle as well as a bath. On the other side of the landing there were two further bedrooms. It wasn't her idea of a tied cottage and she could understand that Jenny and Peter would be reluctant to lose it. She quickly brushed her hair and, picking up the books, returned downstairs.

Peter had cleared the table and was in the kitchen but he came back to the living-room when he heard the children's excited voices. Amy was jumping up and down. 'Look, Daddy, look!'

'Let me see. Ooh, *Orlando the Marmalade Cat*. My favourite. Thank you, Claudia.'

'Silly Daddy, it's *mine*. It *is* mine, isn't it, Claudia?'

'It certainly is, sweetheart. Shall we read some of it? Unless I can help with something, Peter?'

'Amusing the kids would be as useful as anything.'

He returned to the kitchen and Claudia settled on the big settee with Ben and Amy on either side of her. At the other end Jenny was resting with her feet up. Claudia noticed that, in response, her lively face looked strained.

She started to read quietly from *Orlando*, pointing out the charming detail in the pictures. Peter returned to the room and paused, listening for a minute. He caught Claudia's eye and gestured at Jenny. She looked across and saw that Jenny was asleep, the tension smoothed from her face. Peter smiled and Claudia's heart lurched. Now that they were together again she could feel the old easy affection between them, but still Peter exercised his dangerous magic on her.

He returned to his chores and Claudia continued reading until Jenny stirred and announced that it was time for the children to go to bed. Claudia went upstairs with them, helping to prepare them for bed. Then Jenny changed into a pretty flowered smock and Claudia exchanged her sweater for an indigo-blue silk shirt.

Downstairs the meal was almost ready and Jenny began to set the table in the small dining-room. It was a charming room, particularly now, lit by a soft lamp over the table. The polished table, chairs and Welsh dresser were antique pieces. Old plates shone on the dresser and there were half-a-dozen of Jenny's small watercolours in an alcove near the door. Claudia's glance moved to the matching alcove on the other side of the stone fireplace and her heart stood still.

Peter's portrait of her. She had almost forgotten it, but now, lit from below, it blazed like a beacon from her past. He had pictured her wearing an emerald-green dress and standing behind a wing-chair, her arms resting along its back. Her hair, longer then, was loosely caught back, her hazel eyes gazed steadily at the artist.

Although she was too far away to read it, Claudia knew there was an inscription above Peter's signature. It read, *Claudia on the Wing*. A little joke, he had said, a play on words. She had leant on the wing of the chair and he had succeeded in capturing a moment of repose in her mercurial flight.

Jenny had moved to look at it with her. 'I suppose you should have had it, really, but we both love it so. It's definitely Peter's best work.'

Claudia said quietly, 'I'd almost forgotten it.'

'What, forgotten my *magnum opus?* How could you, Claudia?' Peter had come in to join them. His tone was light, but his eyes as they met Claudia's were sombre.

'You always made me look fat when you painted me,' Jenny complained.

'But very appealing. Now, does anybody want any dinner? I've been slaving over a hot stove for hours.'

'It smells terrific. Can I help with anything?' Claudia asked.

'If you'll just bring the plates. We're drinking cider, I hope that's OK. I opened a bottle for the casserole.'

Peter fetched the casserole and vegetables and served them while Jenny poured the cider.

'The children are adorable,' Claudia said.

'Of course,' Peter said proudly. 'What did you expect?'

'Did you say they go to nursery school?'

'Yes, in Marling. It's only a small village, but, fortunately, it has a nursery school. It's good for them to mix with other kids as we're a bit isolated here. Then, next September, when Amy is five, she starts infant school in Otterburn. If we're still here,' Peter added.

'How long have you lived here?'

'Almost two years. There was an elderly lady,

Mrs Cunningham, living here then – at the big house, I mean. She was a friend of our family doctor. She needed someone to do a bit of work on the place and drive her about occasionally. It seemed ideal for us. The cottage is very comfortable and the place is perfect to bring up young children.'

Peter's answer was reasonable, Claudia conceded, but it left questions unanswered. Why had he thrown up his job? Why, after their lengthy training, had he and Jenny chosen to become what sounded like domestic servants? Had Jenny's distress during their phone conversation anything to do with it?

But, as they ate the delicious meal, the atmosphere was relaxed and convivial and Claudia hoped that her arrival would put Jenny's worries out of her mind for a while.

'Have you managed to do much painting since you've been here? Was that part of the plan?'

Claudia thought a glance flickered between Peter and Jenny.

'That was the idea,' Peter answered, 'but we're kept pretty busy one way and another. Perhaps when the kids are older. But tell us what you've been doing. We hear scraps of news from time to time.'

'Oh, a bit of this and a bit of that. It's called diversifying.'

'You disappeared so suddenly when your father died,' Jenny said. 'Why didn't you come to us?'

'Claudia did come to tell us, Jenny, you know that,' Peter said. 'You were out at the time.'

'It was very quick. We had no warning,' Claudia said. 'I think I was in shock. I stayed with my mother for a short while, but I got word of an interesting job in London and she forced me to take it.'

'What was the job?' Peter asked.

'I was working for a greetings-card firm, selecting fine-art images to be used on their cards. It was fun, but I really missed the north, the space and the beauty. So, after about eighteen months, I moved to Durham where my mother is teaching.'

'Do you live with her?' Jenny asked.

'No, I have my own flat, but I see her pretty often. Anyway, in London I had been doing some watercolours and small needlework pictures that sold well. I made some contacts. Then I did some designs for scarves and costume jewellery; a fashion company liked them and put out a small production line.'

'And the writing?'

'I review craft shows and exhibitions, draw attention to people who are doing interesting work. Sometimes I lecture or demonstrate on craft courses. I enjoy the variety, you don't get bored with one thing and I get to travel a bit.'

'It sounds great,' Jenny said, almost wistfully. 'Such industry! You're an example to us all. But I spy a yawning gap. What about the personal bits? What about Meaningful Relationships?'

'Sorry, nothing to report in that line.'

'How about meaningless ones, then?'

Claudia laughed. 'Oh, sure, masses of those. Haven't you heard about us girls on the road?'

'I wish you could find someone.' Jenny's face was earnest and pink from the cider or the glowing fire. 'Do you remember, when we were at school, we would talk about our kids playing together?'

'My God, Jenny,' Peter said shortly. 'You get really maudlin when you drink. Don't pry into Claudia's private life.'

Jenny looked at him in surprise. 'I'm sorry, Claudia,' she said, chastened. 'We always used to confide. I'd forgotten it was so long—'

Claudia reached across and squeezed her hand. 'When I have anything to confide you will be the first to hear it.'

Peter said, 'I'm sorry I yelled, Jen. Now, is anyone for pud?'

Claudia groaned. 'After that meal? You must be joking!'

'It's only icecream,' Jenny said, 'and you know you never put on weight.'

Peter cleared their plates and returned with the icecream. After a minute Claudia said, 'I take it this Mrs Cunningham isn't here now?'

'No, unfortunately,' Peter said grimly. 'She left last September. She couldn't face another winter here. She's nearly eighty and the house was much too big for her. She went south to live with her daughter.'

'Is it empty now?'

'It was bought three months ago.'

'So what's the new owner like?'

'Boorish, arrogant, rude—' Jenny catalogued.

'Be fair,' Peter cautioned. 'He's perfectly civil.'

Jenny snorted. 'He hardly speaks to me.'

'Mrs Cunningham was very sweet, you see,' Peter explained. 'Kind and thoughtful. So this man does come as a bit of a contrast.'

'He reminds me of Mr Rochester,' Jenny muttered.

'Before or after the fire?' Claudia enquired.

Jenny went into a fit of giggles and Peter regarded her fondly.

'I suppose he does come over as arrogant. Master of the Big House and that kind of thing.'

'What is all this about the Big House?' Claudia demanded. 'It's positively feudal. You'll be tugging your forelocks next.'

Peter flushed. 'It's surprising how subservient you can get when your family's livelihood depends on the man.'

'I'm sorry, Peter. I didn't realize the situation was like that. Does this man take advantage of your situation?'

'No, he doesn't do that. He just wants us out of the place.'

'He bought the cottage, too?'

'It's all part of the estate. And I can see his point of view. We earned our keep in Mrs Cunningham's time, but he doesn't need us. He doesn't need driving around and he prefers to do the running repairs on the place himself. He even got rid of the woman who cleaned for Mrs Cunningham – said she was prying into his affairs. He's got an obsession with privacy. He threw a man off the premises because he was in the copse with binoculars and he was only birdwatching!'

'Perhaps he's wanted?' Claudia hazarded.

'Not by me,' Jenny giggled.

'He could sell the cottage for a good price,' Peter went on. 'Or he could get a high rent if he let it – even only seasonally. We couldn't afford that sort of money and, if we could, there's no work around here.'

'So what will you do?'

Peter shrugged. 'At present all we can do is keep

a low profile and make ourselves as useful to him as
we can. I don't think he'd turn us out,' he finished,
without much conviction.

Claudia was sickened at the thought of Jenny
and Peter's humiliation. 'Does he have a family?'

'No, he's alone up there,' Jenny answered.
'There was a wife when he looked the place over
prior to buying, but she never arrived here.'

'Perhaps she's locked up in the attic like the first
Mrs Rochester,' Claudia suggested.

'Being married to Mark Stanhope would drive
anyone crazy,' Jenny said. 'But please remember,
Claudia, if you should run into him, we have to
co-exist with him.'

'I'll drop a curtsy,' Claudia promised. 'I'll simper
fetchingly—'

'Just don't get bolshie,' Peter said.

The conversation turned to other things, to old
acquaintances and more carefree times. The fire
settled gently in the hearth as they talked on,
happy in each other's company.

When an unseen clock pinged ten, Peter got to
his feet yawning. Claudia helped him to clear the
table and wash the dishes, then went upstairs
where she washed quickly before getting into bed.

She was very tired, but the unaccustomed silence
kept her wakeful. That and the jumble of emotions
that crowded her mind. Pleasure that the three of
them had so easily re-established their old
intimacy, dismay that Peter could still disturb her
and, above all, shock at her friends' unhappy
situation.

The following morning she woke to the steady
drumming of rain on the window. She looked at
her bedside clock. It was 7.30. Through the wall

she could hear the children's excited whispering
being firmly shushed by Peter.

Smiling to herself, Claudia put on her dressing-
gown. The previous night Jenny had given her
what she termed 'the order of the battle'. Peter
normally left for work at eight o'clock while she
bathed and fed the children, delivering them to the
village nursery school by 9.30 but, in the past few
days, Peter had taken over the job. Claudia had
assured them that she would do it in future and
Jenny was not to stir from her bed.

She glanced in the mirror, running a hairbrush
through her hair, then looked out on to the
landing. Through the open bathroom door she saw
Peter supervising Ben and Amy's teeth-cleaning.

'Lo, Claudia!' Ben yelled, spraying toothpaste
over a wide area.

'Shush!' Amy hissed dramatically. 'Mummy's
asleep.'

'Believe it or not, she is, even with this din going
on,' Peter said. 'I think it's sheer relief at someone
taking things off her shoulders.'

'I can take over now if you want to get off. I'll
take Jenny her breakfast in bed before I leave for
the school.'

'That would be great.' Peter looked at his
offspring dubiously. 'Are you sure you can
manage?'

'Well, I can clean my own teeth. How different
can it be? We'll be fine. Jenny gave me the
rundown last night and the children are going to
be angels.' Claudia circled her hands around Ben's
neck. *'Aren't you?'*

He squealed delightedly. 'I'm always *quite* an
angel,' Amy said smugly.

'I would like to get away if you're sure you'll be OK. Mark has been in a foul mood lately.'

He went downstairs. Claudia finished the children's toilet, then, when they were settled at the breakfast table, she hastily washed and dressed and took a cup of tea to Jenny.

As she entered the room, Jenny surfaced sleepily. 'Hi. This is great. Just like the old days in Waterloo Place!'

'I seem to remember it was more often you bringing tea to me. I'm sure you're still in credit. How are you feeling?'

Jenny heaved herself up against the pillows. 'Fine. How are the brats behaving?'

'As good as gold, but I'd better get back to them. Can I get you some breakfast?'

'I think I'll snuggle down again for a few minutes. When you get back, we'll talk, Claudia.'

'Sure. I'll bring the children up to say goodbye before we leave.'

Claudia ran back downstairs and grabbed some coffee and toast for herself while Ben and Amy finished eating. Then she sponged their faces and took them up to say goodbye to Jenny. She helped them into their bright oilskins, turned up the collar of her reefer jacket and shepherded the children through the rain to the car.

She cleared the windscreen, set the car in motion and bumped slowly towards the gateposts, turned between them and headed for the village. In a few moments it came into view, a rather depressing double row of terraced cottages with a small general store halfway down the right-hand side.

'Into the shop!' Ben and Amy chorused and Claudia, forewarned by Jenny, swung the car into an entry immediately preceding the shop.

The village street had been deserted but, in this large courtyard, four young women waited with half-a-dozen small children. At the rear, in what had probably once been stabling, a brightly painted door announced the Stepping Stones Nursery School.

Claudia got out of the car and Amy and Ben ran to join friends. One of the women approached Claudia smiling. 'Hello. I'm Karen Dean. I run this place. Is Jenny all right?'

'Yes, but I'm staying with her for a few days to give her a hand.'

'That's good. I know things are difficult for them right now. I'm glad Jenny has a friend with her.'

'Do I just leave Ben and Amy?'

'Oh, yes. They're no trouble. Just pick them up at 12.30. In out of the rain, children!'

Claudia hugged Amy and Ben, got back into her car and reversed carefully into the road. Soon she was back at the entrance to Brackenfield. She swung between the gateposts taking the turning too wide and felt her front wheels squelch down into the muddy verge.

Swearing lustily, she attempted to reverse back on to the track, but her front wheels spun uselessly, churning up a spray of mud. A low forward gear only succeeded in digging the car in further.

The rain was now torrential. It was impossible to see any distance, but there didn't seem to be anyone about to come to her rescue. Reluctantly she climbed out of the car. The rain lashed her face and plastered her hair to her head. She plodded round to open the boot. She often had packing material in there which, packed behind the wheels,

might give them some grip. She was peering in
hopefully when a furious voice assailed her.

'You there! What do you think you're doing?'

Claudia jumped. A man had appeared from
nowhere and was standing on the drive above her.
Dark and scowling, he looked about seven feet tall.
Her heart sank. It had to be Mr Rochester.

He descended the slope with rapid strides. 'This
is private property. What are you doing here?'

Claudia pushed back her sodden hair, preparing
a curt, yet not bolshie, reply, when the man
stopped short, staring at her. He continued his
perusal for some seconds, then he said, 'Good God
– it's the girl in the picture!'

Three

The carefully crafted retort left Claudia's lips and she stared in her turn. If this was Mark Stanhope he was about thirty years old. His very dark eyes were now marginally less hostile and the hint of a smile tweaked at his long mouth. Beneath a tweed cap Claudia could see damp black curls.

She dashed a raindrop from her nose. 'What did you say?'

'Liddell's lost love. The girl in the picture. The one he keeps the light burning beneath.'

Claudia's cheeks burned. Was it possible that Peter had confided in this man? 'I don't know what you're talking about. Peter did paint my portrait, years ago when we were students together—'

'I know. It's in his dining-room. I often admire it.'

'He painted a lot of portraits. He's done several of Jenny.'

'I've seen some of those, too. They're painted with great affection. But the passion – that's only to be found in *Claudia on the Wing*.'

'You have a vivid imagination, Mr Stanhope. I take it you are Mr Stanhope? As for what I'm doing here – one, I'm staying with the Liddells and, two, I'm trying to get my car unstuck.'

34

She started to drag a sheet of stout cardboard from the boot.

'Get in the car. I'll do that, you're wet enough already.'

Without a word, Claudia handed him the cardboard and got back into the car. Mark Stanhope tucked the cardboard into position behind the wheels. Claudia put the car into reverse and, to her relief, moved back on to the path. Unsmiling, she raised a hand to Stanhope who returned the cardboard to the boot and stood back watching her drive off.

At the cottage, Claudia took off her shoes and carried them, with her wet coat, through to the boiler in the utility room. Going upstairs she met Jenny emerging from the bathroom.

'Claudia, you're absolutely soaked!'

'I know. Would it be possible to have a shower? I only had time for a lick-and-a-promise earlier.'

'Of course. I was just going to have breakfast. I'll wait till you come down.'

Claudia stripped off her wet clothes and showered, changing into dry trousers and socks. She wrapped a towel round her hair and went downstairs to join Jenny.

'I thought you were going to have a lie-in.'

Jenny put bread in the toaster and made a fresh pot of coffee. 'It isn't easy for mothers of young children to stay in bed. We get programmed. How did you manage to get so wet?'

'The car got stuck by the gate and I had to plough around a bit.'

'Hard luck. Did you have much trouble getting it out?'

'No, your landlord came to my rescue.'

'Oh?' Jenny paused in the act of piling toast on to a plate. 'What did he have to say?'

Claudia rubbed at her hair, the towel concealing her face. Stanhope's remarks about the portrait were clearly inadmissible. She said, 'He told me I was trespassing and asked what I was doing there.'

'Oh, dear. Was he angry?'

'He calmed down when I said I was staying here. Then he stuck some cardboard that I had behind my wheels and I got off.'

'What did you think of him?'

Claudia shrugged. 'Pretty bad-tempered, but he was soaked with rain. Anyway, I don't suppose I shall see much of him.'

Accepting a cup of coffee, Claudia detected an uncomfortable expression on her friend's face. 'Jenny? I don't have to see much of him, do I?'

'Why? It sounds as though you quite hit it off.'

'We didn't "hit it off", believe me. He was only anxious for me to stop chewing up his park. Are you keeping something from me?'

'It's only that, once in a while, he asks me to go up to do some typing for him. It's something else we can do to make ourselves useful.'

'And?'

'Well, I did think, if he asked while you were here, you might have gone in my place. He gets a bit impatient with my efforts and you're a much better typist than I am.'

'You're suggesting I go temping for the man?'

'He probably won't ask while you're here, he doesn't very often. Forget I mentioned it. Partly I get nervous because I keep expecting him to ask when we're going to leave the cottage.'

There was a pause while Jenny sipped her

coffee. Then she said, 'Jenny, how did you get into this position?'

'We told you. Mrs Cunningham sold up—'

'I mean before that. Why did you come here at all? Why did Peter give up teaching?'

'It was fine at first, while Mrs Cunningham was here,' Jenny said stubbornly. 'It was just what we wanted.'

'Since when? I know it's none of my business, but I never heard you make plans of that sort. I thought Peter enjoyed teaching.'

Jenny gave her attention to chasing a crumb round her plate. At last she said, 'Peter didn't want you to know, but he's been ill.'

'Why wouldn't he want me to know?'

Jenny continued as though Claudia hadn't spoken. 'Two years ago he was involved in a car accident. It wasn't his fault, but the young man in the other car was killed.'

'How dreadful!'

'What made it worse was that he was a pupil of Peter's. His prize pupil. He was very excited about him, he thought he had great promise. He'd been given the car on his eighteenth birthday two months previously. Peter had just left college when David came out of another exit – a concealed drive they were supposed to treat with great caution – and smashed into him.'

'Was Peter hurt?'

'Only slightly. Chest bruising and some damaged ligaments in his hand. But emotionally he was in a terrible state.'

'But if it wasn't his fault—'

'I know and he knew – with his conscious mind – but he became very depressed. He couldn't get his hand working properly, although the hospital said it had mended. He couldn't bring himself to return to college. They called it post trauma shock syndrome. He couldn't help it, Claudia. He wanted to look after us—'

'I know that, Jenny. And it's certainly nothing to be ashamed of, being devastated by a tragedy you've caused, even innocently.'

After a moment Jenny resumed. 'Things went from bad to worse. The college was getting under-standably impatient and Peter was dreadfully unhappy. Then our doctor thought of this place. He was tactful – said artists often took a sabbatical to do some work – and we moved in from our rented flat.

'It wasn't easy at first. It wasn't work either of us had been used to, but Mrs Cunningham was very kind. The children loved it and, after a time, we started to enjoy the life, too. Peter got much better, he was thinking of getting down to some painting and we embarked on the new baby. Then Mrs Cunningham decided to sell up—'

'Enter Mark Stanhope,' Claudia prompted.

'Exactly. You couldn't find a greater contrast. Something's bugging the man. He's unhappy – I recognize it from Peter – but it doesn't make it any easier to get along with him.'

Claudia snorted. 'He's just foul-tempered if you ask me.' She reached across and took Jenny's hand. 'Oh, Jenny, I wish you had told me about this before.'

Jenny sniffed. 'Peter didn't want you to know.'

'What will you do?'

'Peter is looking for a job starting in September. I don't know if he'll have any luck. I just hope Mark will let us stay until he does.'

'Surely he will?'

'It would lose him a season's bookings if he did decide to let it. And now, with me *hors de combat* in this stupid way, Peter is frantically worried.'

'I could stay for a while,' Claudia said slowly, 'if that would help. I mean I could work from here. I'd have to go back to Durham occasionally, but, apart from that, I could be here.'

'That would be wonderful.' Jenny's eyes were bright with tears. 'It would be such a weight off Peter's mind.'

'That's settled then. And if the summons comes from the Big House I shall hasten to obey.'

'Claudia, would you?'

'I will even grovel.'

Jenny beamed moistly. 'Now, that's something I'd like to see!'

'Now, will you retire to your couch and prepare me a list of duties while I tidy up?'

Jenny got to her feet. In the doorway she turned back to Claudia. 'Why did you really leave for London so suddenly?'

'Can't fool you, huh? Well – if it's confession time – there was a man. No one you knew. I thought I was in love with him, but he was married. The best thing seemed to be to get right away.'

'I wish you'd told me. Sometimes I used to think it had something to do with me.'

Claudia smiled at her. 'Of course, it hadn't anything to do with you.'

The remainder of the morning was spent in household chores. At noon Peter came in and had a sandwich with them. Jenny related Claudia's meeting with Mark Stanhope, and, like hers, his immediate reaction was whether Stanhope had been annoyed.

Claudia was irritated that her friends' peace of mind appeared to hang on the man's mood. 'Are you forbidden visitors?'

'Of course not. He didn't object anyway. I saw him an hour ago. He was asking questions about you.'

Jenny looked up from her sandwich. 'It's not like him to show an interest in anything. What did he say?'

'Just how long Claudia was staying. Where she lived. Whether we were old friends.'

Jenny's eyes widened. 'We-ell, you've struck a spark in that flinty heart!'

'He was only making conversation,' Peter said shortly.

'He doesn't make conversation—'

'I'll go for the kids, I've got time.' Peter changed the subject. 'It's stopped raining, Claudia, we could take a walk around the place this afternoon, if you'd like.'

'Is that all right with you, Jenny?'

'Of course.'

Peter left and Claudia cleared the dishes. She hoped that Peter was going to be able to keep a rein on his feelings. To anyone less trusting than Jenny his annoyance over Mark Stanhope's apparent interest in her would have been obvious and she resolved to tackle him about it when she got the chance.

In a few minutes he was back with the children, each carrying a large still-damp painting which they showed proudly to Claudia.

'They're both very good, darlings,' she pronounced having given Ben's field of woolly sheep and Amy's self-portrait her serious attention. 'You both have Mummy and Daddy's talent.'

Well pleased, they sat down to their lunch and Jenny, having found a pair of wellington boots to fit Claudia, produced a pile of mending to work on while they had their nap.

Claudia put on the boots and her jacket and went outside with Peter. The rain still held off and a hazy sun was just visible through the clouds.

'We'll have a walk around the grounds, then go up to the house. Mark is going into Otterburn for some stuff, so he won't be there.'

'What are you working on at present?'

'We're repairing the walls round the other two cottages. The sheep keep getting in and making a hell of a mess. It's a drystone wall which isn't as simple a job as it looks. It's falling down as fast as we put it up.'

They were climbing uphill away from the lane towards the curve of the river. On the farther bank half-a-dozen cows had joined the sheep to stare at the human company.

Claudia said, 'Do the sheep belong to Stanhope?'

'No, he rents out the grazing.'

She looked at the swirling river. 'It's very fast – and so near the cottage. Aren't you afraid for the children?'

'We were at first, but they understand now that they mustn't go near it. There's a strong fence between us.'

They skirted the river and walked on to the brow of the hill where they turned and looked back. The fields folding together were a dazzling green, snaked through by the brown river. Directly below them lay the Liddells' cottage and, a short distance along the lane, the shining slate roofs of the village. Here and there were dark clusters of trees. To their left a larger coppice half-hid Brackenfield House.

'I wonder why he lives alone in such a big place,' Claudia said. 'And why the passion for privacy. Maybe he does have a secret.'

Peter leant back against a tree. He gazed at Claudia as though trying to imprint her features on his memory. 'Everyone has a secret.'

Claudia looked away. 'I hope not a guilty one.'

'There hasn't been a day that I haven't thought about you—'

'Peter, don't—'

'I'm trying not to. I swore to myself I wouldn't rake everything up.'

'Everything? It wasn't so very much.'

'You ran away. I couldn't trace you.'

'That was the idea. You know it was the only way.'

'I know. But I loved you so much.'

'And I loved you, but I loved Jenny, too. She was my friend.' She turned away decisively. 'This isn't the time for this, Peter.' She looked across to Brackenfield. 'Can we get to the house from here?'

'There's a path along the crest.' He put out a restraining hand. 'Claudia—' But she had moved swiftly away.

'What does Stanhope do for a living?' she asked over her shoulder.

'Why are you so interested in him?'

'I'm not particularly. I just wondered what he could do from here.'

'He's a boatbuilder.'

'A boatbuilder?' It wasn't what she had expected. 'Here in the north?'

'No, on the south coast.'

'This is a long distance to function from.'

'Perhaps he's sold up the business. He doesn't talk much about it.'

They walked on for a few minutes in silence until the path they were on skirted the trees and they found themselves at the back of the house. From the rear the house looked bare and uninhabited, with several of its windows uncurtained. The gravelled area behind it needed weeding and the outbuildings were in need of repair.

'It doesn't look lived-in,' Claudia said.

'Mrs Cunningham only used a handful of rooms for the last few years. Most of the others were furnished, though.'

Claudia indicated the decaying outbuildings. 'There seems to be plenty of work to be done.'

'Of course, there is, but Mark doesn't seem to have his heart in it. Maybe if his wife turned up—'

They made their way round the side of the house. Through one window Claudia saw a room furnished as an office or study with bookshelves lining the walls and a handsome mahogany desk. At the front of the house there were two deep sash windows on either side of the front door. On the left they looked into a finely furnished sitting-room, to the right an elegant dining-room.

'At least he has good taste,' Claudia observed. 'He has some very nice pieces of furniture.'

They completed the circuit with a window on the east side that appeared to belong to a breakfast-room. On this side there was an overgrown garden with paved walks, sagging trellises and a small summerhouse.

'He certainly needs some help.' Claudia peered through the dirty windows of the summerhouse at piled garden furniture. 'It's pitiful. This should be a family home.' She turned away and a straggling rambler rose caught in her hair.

'Ouch!' She put up a hand to untwine the thorny strand.

'Keep still.' Peter started to help her, then one hand moved to stroke her cheek. His eyes, inches away, locked with hers.

'You're making it worse!' Claudia snapped. Quickly and painfully she dragged her hair free. Peter's hands dropped to her waist. There was a small noise behind them and, whirling round, they saw Mark Stanhope watching them with cold amusement.

'Oh, there you are, Peter,' he said... 'Playing house?'

Peter backed away from Claudia. 'I was showing Claudia the place. I hope that's OK?'

'Of course. You must make time to entertain Miss James.'

'I'm not here to be entertained—'

He ignored her interruption. 'Would you take a look at that aggregate in the boot, Peter? See if you think it's the right stuff.'

'Sure.' Peter cast a doubtful glance at Claudia, then brushed past Mark on the narrow path. Claudia made to follow, but Mark was barring her way. Short of pushing him bodily aside there was nothing to do but remain.

'So – what do you think of my house?'

'Well – I'd have to say it's a little—'

She wilted beneath his bleak gaze.

'It lacks something, you think? A family, perhaps? Are you an advocate of the family, Miss James?'

Claudia's cheeks flamed. If his words were a comment on hers – that Brackenfield should be a family house – he had been watching them before Peter's attempted embrace.

She said stiffly, 'I'm here to help with the family – with the children. Jenny isn't well, she has to rest – so she called on me.'

'She called – or Peter?'

'Jenny called. Peter didn't approve, I understand.'

'I find that hard to believe.'

'I'm really not interested in what you believe, Mr Stanhope.' Oh lord, bolshie already, she thought, catching sight of Peter's horrified face over Stanhope's shoulder.

'Yes, that seems to be right,' Peter said.

'Good, we'll make a start tomorrow.' He finally stood aside to allow Claudia to pass. 'It was nice meeting, Miss James.'

Claudia nodded curtly and followed Peter with what dignity she could muster in her loose-fitting wellingtons.

'Sorry, Peter,' she said ruefully. 'I did try, but the man is impossible. I'd better keep out of his way.'

'What started it?'

'He believes we're having an affair.'

'What?' He stopped and stared at her.

'Well, what did you expect? Peter, you've got to stop – giving anyone the wrong impression. I couldn't bear Jenny to be hurt.'

'Do you think I could?'

'I know you couldn't. Stanhope wouldn't say anything to her, would he?'

'I'm sure he wouldn't upset her. He seems to like Jenny, despite what she says about him.'

They struck off downhill across the grass and soon reached the cottage. Claudia was tired after the day's exertions and wasn't sorry to find the children still napping.

Jenny looked up smiling as they came in. 'Have you done the tour?'

Claudia flopped on to the settee. 'Where every prospect pleases and only man is vile,' she quoted.

'Does that mean you met Mark?'

'He snuck up on us while we were snooping round the house.'

'Did he object?'

'He didn't seem to. I don't think he cares for me, though.'

'Oh, pity. I was hoping you might soften him up. He's terrific looking, you must admit.'

'A bit unsubtle for me. If you're an Ashley Wilkes lady you're never going to understand the appeal of Rhett Butler. Anyway, his wife can soften him up.'

'Word around the village is that she up and left him.'

'I don't wonder.' Claudia yawned widely. 'I'm bushed. It must be the country air.'

'Oh, Claudia, I'm sorry – we're wearing you out. Put your feet up. Put the kettle on, Peter.'

Peter did as he was bade, soon returning with a tray of tea and biscuits and they enjoyed a peaceful half-hour before the children came downstairs to find out that they were missing. Later, they went outside to play, then Claudia read to them until it was time for their supper. After it she helped Jenny to bath and put them to bed while Peter again prepared their own meal.

They had just finished eating when, at eight

o'clock, the phone rang. Peter went to answer it.
They heard his curt responses from the living-
room. He returned to the dining-room looking
annoyed.

'Who was it?' Jenny asked.

'It was Mark.'

'Mark! What did he want?'

Peter banged down a serving dish he had been
clearing. 'He says he wants you to go up and do
some work for him tomorrow. As he knows very
well that you aren't fit, I suspect he is hoping that
Claudia will offer to go in your place.'

'I don't think he'd assume that,' Jenny said
innocently. 'How would he know she can use faxes
and word-processors and things? She might be
useless at it.'

'Does Claudia look as though she's useless at
anything?'

'Thanks for the vote of confidence,' Claudia said.
'As it happens, I am reasonably competent, but it's
not a prospect I view with any pleasure.'

'I can go,' Jenny said. 'It's not strenuous. So – if
Peter is correct – Mark is in for a disappointment.'

'Well – if you're sure,' Claudia said doubtfully.
'Let's see how you feel in the morning.'

The subject wasn't mentioned again as they had
their coffee and sat talking until bedtime, but, for
Claudia at least, it hung over the evening like an
ominous cloud.

The following morning she woke to the murmur
of voices from below. She washed and dressed
quickly and went downstairs to find Peter giving
the children their breakfast.

'Sorry, Peter, I slept later then I meant to.'

'There's plenty of time. Could you just keep an

eye on this pair while you're having your breakfast?'

Claudia sat down at the table and buttered some toast. 'How is Jenny?'

Peter looked worried. 'Not very well. She had a lot of back pain in the night.'

'That doesn't sound good.'

'The baby is jumping up and down inside her tummy,' Ben informed them through a mouthful of cereal.

Claudia smiled. 'Is she awake now?' she asked Peter.

'She's dozing. I won't disturb her. Could you take the kids to school?'

'Don't worry about things here. What about the work for Stanhope?'

'I'll just tell him Jenny isn't well – period.'

Claudia said reluctantly, 'If there's any problem, you can tell him I'll help if I can.'

Peter smiled the sweet smile that still jolted her heart. 'Thanks, Claudia. I'll try to be back here by twelve to collect Amy and Ben.'

He kissed the children and departed. Claudia finished her own hasty breakfast, saw that the children had finished theirs and helped them into their coats.

Outside the cottage a sprinkling of yellow crocuses caught the pale sunshine. Claudia delivered the children to their schoolroom, then, leaving the car, walked the length of the village street. The excursion took less than five minutes. There was little attractive about the rows of plain houses, although the scenery behind them was spectacular. She bought a newspaper and drove back to Brackenfield, negotiating the gateposts carefully. No irate owner appeared to yell at her this morning.

At the cottage there was still no sound from Jenny's room and Claudia sat down with her paper. At ten o'clock, just as she was about to go up to see whether Jenny wanted anything, the phone rang.

She glanced up the staircase. There was no sign of Jenny stirring so she picked up the receiver. 'Claudia James here.'

'Oh, Miss James,' Mark Stanhope's slow, deep voice was unmistakable. 'I was expecting Jenny this morning. Do you know whether she has left?'

Claudia bit back her irritation. 'Jenny isn't well. Didn't Peter tell you?'

'I haven't seen Peter this morning.' There was a pause. 'That's unfortunate.'

'Yes,' Claudia agreed, deliberately misunder-standing. 'We're quite concerned about her.'

'Oh, yes, of course. I'm sorry to hear it. Well, I suppose it will have to wait.' There was a second pause. 'I don't suppose you would be willing to help, Miss James?'

'It's not really my line of work,' Claudia said airily. She glanced up the staircase to see Jenny watching her anxiously. 'But if you're really stranded – and I'm able to leave Jenny—'

'I'd be very grateful.'

'I'll come up when I can manage it then.' She replaced the receiver and looked up at Jenny. 'I think you could call it a draw. I agreed, but I made him beg a little bit. Why are you out of bed, Jen? You look proper poorly.'

'I heard the phone.' Jenny sat down suddenly on the top stair. 'I thought you were going to annoy him.'

'*Annoy him*? Good grief, what sort of a brute is he? Peter should have told him firmly that you weren't well enough. But don't worry about it. Go back to bed and I'll bring you some breakfast. Then, when I'm good and ready, I'll stroll up to the Big House. It's time Mr High-and-Mighty Stanhope met his match.'

Four

Claudia persuaded Jenny to bed, then prepared a breakfast tray and took it to her. She tidied the kitchen and bathroom before going to her own room where she considered the selection of clothes she had brought with her. Power-dressing wasn't feasible given the limited choice available and, in any case, she didn't want to look like the head of Stanhope's typing pool. In the end she decided on her dusty-pink cords and a white polo-necked sweater. Peter had cleaned her muddy shoes and she slipped them on with her reefer jacket and picked up her bag.

Outside, the sun had strengthened and there was a light breeze. Claudia decided to walk up to the house both for exercise and to underline the non-urgency of Mark Stanhope's summons. Deliberately she stooped to examine a quite commonplace shrub. As she straightened up she saw him waiting for her in the doorway.

He continued to watch her as she approached. As she drew near he said, 'I hope this hasn't put you out.'

She shrugged ungraciously. 'If you're really stuck—'

He led the way into the house. The big square

51

hall had walls of Tuscan red with a number of white-painted doors leading off it. Unlike the outside of the house, the interior was newly and tastefully decorated. He opened a door on the left and they entered the small study. In addition to the mahogany desk there was a smaller desk out of view of the window and, on it, a small computer and a typewriter.

Stanhope picked up a dictaphone from the big desk. 'I dictated a few letters earlier. Could you type them up for me? I do understand this isn't your usual sort of work—'

Claudia slipped out of her jacket. 'It isn't Jenny's usual sort of work either.'

'You can type?'

'Just self-taught, but I'm fairly fast.'

Now that they were together in the small room he seemed almost self-conscious. 'The addresses are with each letter. I think you'll find it straight-forward, but there is some technical stuff in a couple of them – specifications and so on. If you have any problems with them I'll be around the house somewhere.'

He left the room and Claudia cleared a space at the desk and sat down. She took some stationery from a box on the desk. Good quality pale-blue quarto with a darker blue heading. *Mark Stanhope Boats. Welsea. Millinghurst.* She wound a sheet into the machine and flipped on the dictaphone.

She gave a little start as Stanhope's disembodied voice came from the dictaphone, then set to work. It was important to her to be both swift and accurate and the work gave her little trouble. The dictation was impeccable, the right speed, with no hesitation or back tracking. The technical matter was lucidly set out. There were five letters and all of them dealt with boats in the process of building – dimensions, fittings, pricing, legislation. Claudia wondered again how Stanhope could function at such a distance from his base.

She had just started on the last letter when he came into the room carrying a cup of coffee.

'I thought you might like this.'

She looked over her shoulder. 'Thank you. Actually I'm almost finished.'

She thought he looked disappointed. 'Already?' He put the cup down beside her and picked up the completed letters, sitting at the second desk to read them. 'These are fine. Perfect.' He scrawled a decisive signature at the foot of each.

Claudia sipped her coffee. 'It must be difficult to work so far from your business.'

'It's a bit frustrating at times. I find myself longing to see how the craft are coming along, to feel the timber; but I get down there pretty often and I have a very good manager.'

She wanted to ask him why he had moved, but didn't want to risk appearing intrusive. He must have sensed the unspoken question for he said, 'I'd been looking for a place with space and privacy. That's not possible in the south. It would be fiendishly expensive and very hard to get away from the social round. Anyway, I like the north.'

'Did you know this area?'

'Not well. My wife and I spent a couple of holidays just over the border. What about you? You're not a true-born northerner, are you?'

'No. Only by adoption. I was six years old when my father's firm relocated to Newcastle.'

'That's where you live now?'

'No, I'm in Durham now.'

'A beautiful city.'

'Yes, it is.' Claudia put down her cup. Mark Stanhope was relaxed – almost friendly. Through the window she could see a stretch of crumbling wall. 'There's a good deal that needs doing on the property,' she ventured.

He looked at her wryly. 'I gathered yesterday that that was your opinion.'

'I wouldn't call it a well-kept secret.'

'You're right. But it was a case of priorities. The interior needed to be decorated first and the weather has been too bad to do a lot to the outside. However, it's improving now so I can get stuck in. I've plenty of time on my hands.'

Claudia cleared her throat. 'It must be useful having Peter here.'

'To be frank, I prefer to call in professionals as I need them.'

'But why? Peter must be something of a jack-of-all-trades by now.'

'I wouldn't include drystone walling among his trades.'

'Perhaps not. That's a specialized skill—' She broke off. His expression had changed, his eyes now cold and distant.

'The Liddells have recruited you to their cause, I see.'

'Naturally they've told me about their worries and it seems such a practical solution. You agree there's a lot of work here – plus they can act as caretakers when you're away. It was a successful arrangement with the last owner.'

'But I'm not an elderly lady. I'm perfectly capable of running the place without full-time help. As far as I am concerned I bought a vacant property and that's the way I want it. I'm sorry,' he said in the face of Claudia's scowl, 'but it's not my responsibility to provide for Peter's family.'

Claudia did not reply. She turned back to the typewriter and attacked the final letter in a furious burst of speed. She ripped it out of the machine, handed it to Stanhope and picked up her jacket.

He took the letter without looking at it. 'I'm sorry we can't see eye-to-eye over this.' When Claudia still made no response, he said, 'Well – thank you for your help.'

'It was nothing.' Claudia put on her jacket, picked up her bag and stalked from the room, Mark at her heels. She reached the front door ahead of him and flung it open. Peter was sitting in his car on the drive. Claudia wrenched open the passenger door and dropped into the seat beside him.

He said, 'I just dropped the kids off at home. I thought I'd come up and save you a walk.'

'Thanks, Peter, that was thoughtful.'

He looked at her. 'Are you OK?'

At the front door Mark was watching them. Claudia smiled fondly at Peter. 'I'm fine.' As he turned the car down the drive she added less warmly, 'I'd like to know why you landed me with that. I thought you were going to tell him that Jenny wasn't well.'

'I couldn't find him. When I finally ran him to earth he'd already phoned you. How did it go?'

'All right. It was only a few letters for typing. They didn't seem particularly urgent to me.'

'What did he have to say?'

'Not much.' Claudia couldn't bring herself to

repeat Stanhope's discouraging remarks on the Liddells' future. 'He left me alone to get on with it.'

They arrived at the cottage to find Jenny resting on the settee while the children played at the kitchen table. Claudia reassured her that everything had gone smoothly at Brackenfield, then helped Peter to prepare the lunch. After they had eaten he returned to work, Jenny was persuaded back to bed and the children went upstairs for their nap.

Left alone, Claudia cleared the table and washed the dishes. As she worked she thought over the morning's events. She couldn't see that she had done any harm in speaking to Mark Stanhope as she had. It might bring home to him how an outsider viewed his behaviour. Why was he so determined to get rid of the Liddells anyway? That apart, he seemed to be a reasonable – and, she had to admit – a very attractive man. It could be simply financial – that he needed to rent or sell the cottage. But, if that was the case, why had he embarked on such a costly and impractical relocation? She wondered why she had omitted to ask him when his wife planned to join him. It was an obvious and innocent question.

But Mark Stanhope's affairs had no interest for her except where they affected Jenny and Peter. She finished her chores and curled up on the settee with her book until the children came downstairs, then amused them until Jenny joined them. Soon after, Peter came in and, after the children had had their supper and gone to bed, he and Claudia prepared the dinner and all three spent a pleasant evening talking and watching television.

The next three days followed a similar pattern.

Claudia wasn't summoned to Brackenfield again and only once glimpsed Mark Stanhope in the distance. She managed to snatch a little time each day to do some of her own work and, her creative fingers painfully deprived, she begged an old dress from Jenny which she could cut up and sewed into dolls' clothes, demonstrating some simple stitches for the child to copy.

The rain of the first morning returned, pouring down relentlessly, masking the view and turning the ground into a quagmire. Claudia began to feel the onset of claustrophobia. Her days had always been filled with a variety of activities, people and places – now, at times, the cottage almost resembled a prison. When things got too oppressive she donned Jenny's wellingtons and a borrowed raincoat and took herself for long walks over the fields.

On the morning of the sixth day she woke with a feeling that something was different. She couldn't have said what it was. The light on her walls? A sound? She only felt uneasily that something was amiss.

She looked at the clock by her bedside. It was seven o'clock. She got out of bed and went over to the window, pulling aside the curtain. She stared in amazement at the sight that met her eyes. The river had almost doubled its width. Always fast-flowing, it now raced along, bearing with it a cargo of broken branches and other debris. The livestock on the opposite bank stood back and watched its progress with lowered heads. As Claudia looked little tongues of brown water began to snake beneath the fence at the bottom of the garden.

She hesitated. Was there cause for immediate

concern? She wondered if anybody else was awake.
Slipping on her dressing-gown she quietly opened
her bedroom door to see Peter coming up the
stairs.

'Peter, have you seen the river?'

'I've been looking at it. Can I come into your
room?'

Claudia led the way to the window. 'Will it come
much higher? Will it reach the cottage?'

Peter watched the torrent for a moment,
frowning. 'We should be all right here. The garden
rises quite sharply. It was higher than this last
October. The only worry is, at this time of the year
there's still a lot of snow on the hills to come down.'

Claudia shivered. 'It looks so powerful.'

'It's got hundreds of tons of water rushing into it.
But don't worry, I'm sure we'll stay clear. The
worst that will happen is that we will be cut off
from the house and the village. Last October it cut
a channel along the path to the gate. The ground is
lower there.'

'What about the children going to school?'

'They'd better stay at home. We don't want them
stranded in the village. They're still asleep at
present. I'm going to make some tea. Are you
going back to bed?'

'No.' The reflected silver light sliding across the
walls made Claudia feel tense and nervous. She
followed Peter downstairs to the kitchen, going at
once to the window. Already it seemed to her that
the water had crept further beneath the fence.

Peter brought her a mug of tea. 'I think we
should bring the cars up in front of the cottage.
They'll get bogged down where they are – maybe
even swept away.'

Claudia shivered again. 'I was getting a bit claus-
trophobic as it was,' she confessed.

Peter put an arm around her shoulders, drawing
her nearer. 'Come on, Claudia! Where's your fron-
tier spirit? We've plenty of food in the house and, if
we do get cut off, it will only be for forty-eight hours
at most.'

Claudia disengaged herself gently. She sat down
near the stove with her tea. The idea crept into her
head that she might make a dash for home for a
couple of days. She wouldn't be required to take the
children to-and-from school. On the other hand
Jenny might need her help if they were to be
underfoot all day, or if there was any sort of
emergency. She was cursing her tender conscience
when Jenny looked round the door, flushed and
sleepy in her pink dressing-gown.

'I thought I heard someone down here.' She
yawned. 'Are the kids still asleep?'

'They were a few minutes ago. The river's rising
fast,' Peter said. 'Claudia thinks we should start
building an ark.'

Jenny plodded to the window. 'Good lord, it *has*
come up in the night! We'll probably be safe,
though, Claudia. It's been this high before.'

'Higher,' Peter put in.

'Yes, last October in the gales it was higher.'

'Should we keep the children at home?' Peter
asked her.

'Oh, I think so, don't you? And out of the garden,
too. Thank heaven you're here to lend a hand,
Claudia.'

With a faint twinge of regret Claudia saw her
chance of escape disappear. She said, 'I think I hear
them stirring. I'll go up and see what they're up to.'

Leaving Peter and Jenny at the window, she ran upstairs. In the children's room she found Amy kneeling on her bed gazing out of the window at the swollen river. Ben, she saw with dismay, was hauling a small boat from his toy chest.

Amy dragged her eyes from the window. 'Look Claudia, how fast the river is going!'

'Going to sail my boat,' Ben announced.

'No, you can't do that, Ben. The river would snatch it away and you'd lose it. We'll play with it in the bath,' she promised quickly as Ben's mouth began to tremble. 'We'll have lots of time because Daddy says you don't have to go to school.'

She helped the children into their dressing-gowns and they went downstairs to the kitchen where Peter, infected with siege mentality, was cooking large quantities of comfort food – scrambled eggs and bacon, followed by waffles and syrup. After a leisurely breakfast, Claudia went upstairs to shower and dress. When she returned to the kitchen Peter tossed over her car keys.

'Let's get the cars moved to higher ground while we can. Then I'll pile some sandbags along the fence, they'll protect the garden a bit.'

Claudia put on her jacket and followed him outside. The rain had started again like a thick, soft veil. They sprinted to the cars and Claudia drove hers carefully from the muddy field, following Peter through the gate to park in front of the cottage.

Peter pocketed his keys and came over to her. 'I filled some sandbags last October. They're stored in the shed in case they were needed again.'

'Let me help.'

'You'll get soaked.'

'I'll soon dry off.'

'Well, it would speed things up. They're fairly heavy.'

Peter led the way round the side of the cottage and opened the door of the shed. Inside was a clutter of tools and discarded furniture. Peter cleared a way through to a pile of sandbags against the rear wall. He pulled a wheelbarrow free and, taking an end each, he and Claudia heaved four of the sandbags on to the barrow.

Peter wheeled the barrow down the path to the fence beneath which the water was swirling in in several places.

'This is where it's coming in worst. It's the lowest part.' He tipped the barrow and the sandbags splashed into the water. Hastily he and Claudia dragged them into position against the fence.

When they were finished, he stood back. 'That seems to have done the trick, but I'll get a couple more.'

He turned back to the shed. Claudia had turned to follow when she heard a faint, plaintive cry on the other side of the fence. The top of the fence was above eye level so, holding on to the top, she climbed on to a sandbag and looked over.

Here the racing river was alarmingly close. Most of the livestock had moved back but, right at the water's edge, a single sheep bleated in apparent distress.

'Get back, you stupid animal,' Claudia muttered.

The feeble cry came again, not from the lone ewe, but closer to the fence. Claudia pulled herself higher. A tiny eyot had become detached from the bank and on it, bleating piteously, a lamb was marooned.

'Oh, God!' Claudia gazed at the little creature in dismay. 'Stay there!' she hissed fiercely at it, then jumped down from the fence and raced round the side of the cottage, shouting a terse explanation to Peter deep inside the shed.

She went through the gate and along the hedge. The river was now a frightening sight. It still followed its proper course, but the banks were breaking up and the overspill was spreading rapidly towards Claudia and the lane. She stopped for a moment to assess the situation. The lamb was marooned off the farther bank to the river, its islet cut off from the bank by a narrow, but fast-flowing channel.

Claudia eyed the lamb and it looked back at her, awaiting her next move. She was anxious not to scare it into falling into the main current. It was impossible to judge the depth of the separating channel – the safest move seemed to be to launch herself across it. Making reassuring noises at the animal, she advanced to the nearest point of the bank and leapt for the island. The lamb backed to the furthest edge, bleating loudly, its feet scrabbling in the mud. Claudia lunged forward and grabbed it. As she did so she was aware of two human voices competing with the animal's. Peter's from behind her; Mark Stanhope's, louder, angrier, from the hill above.

Clutching the struggling lamb to her chest she turned round and sat down heavily on the island. Stanhope, his face dark with anger, charged down the hill.

'You idiot! What the hell are you doing?'

Several sharp rejoinders sprang to Claudia's lips but she concentrated on clinging on to the lamb which now appeared teenaged rather than infant. At the same time she noticed that the channel between her and the bank had widened considerably.

Mark reached the water's edge and held out his arm. 'Grab hold of me. You can reach.'

'I can't. I can't let go of the lamb.'

'Stick it under your arm. Quick, the bank is going!'

Glancing swiftly to her right, Claudia saw that the river was now swirling across the hillside to find its own level alongside the path. Peter, jumping about in agitation on the other side of the overspill, added his voice to Mark's.

'Hurry, Claudia, you'll be swept away!'

Realization that she was in danger of being stranded on the wrong side of the river with Mark Stanhope prompted Claudia to action. She struggled to her knees, the lamb clamped beneath her left arm, as Mark stepped into the channel that separated them. The water reached halfway up his thighs, but he grabbed Claudia round the waist and dragged her on to the bank beside him. The lamb gave a powerful kick and leapt for its mother sending Claudia sprawling in the mud.

'Claudia, quick!' Peter's voice was urgent. 'Come on, or you won't make it!'

'Too late.' Mark hauled her none-too-gently to her feet. He smiled at her complacently. 'Look!'

The entire river was rapidly changing its course, cutting her off from Peter and the cottage. But it was still shallow. Claudia attempted to pull away from Mark, but his grip tightened.

'Don't be a fool, you'll never get through there.'

As he spoke the river suddenly burst its banks

and, with a frightening roar, rushed towards the lane. Claudia cast a despairing look at Peter whose own expression was a mixture of chagrin and dismay. She wondered if he was recalling his earlier words which now rang so horribly in her own ears: *'Forty eight hours. It will only be for forty-eight hours at most.'*

Five

She swung round on Mark. 'You did that deliberately.'

'What – parted the waters? Even I don't have quite such an elevated view of myself.'

'You held me back. I could have got to the other side.'

'You could have been swept away.' He raised his voice. 'Don't worry, Peter. I'll look after her!' He took a fresh grip on Claudia's elbow and started to steer her up the hill.

Claudia pushed soaking hair from her face with a muddy hand. 'God, I hate the country! Peter said the water could stay up for forty-eight hours.'

'Then we'll have plenty of time to get to know each other.'

She glared at him. 'I can't believe we're completely cut off. There must be a way round—'

'I assure you there isn't. You'll just have to face the dreadful prospect. Now will you get a move on?' Claudia was still making ineffectual attempts to hang back. 'You'll feel a lot better when you've got those clothes off.'

Momentarily silenced, Claudia plodded after him, slithering on the muddy surface. After a minute, she said, 'You'd have let that lamb drown.'

'It isn't my lamb.'

'Haven't you any concern for anything that's not in your interests?'

'Oh, for heaven's sake, let's postpone the moralizing. The blasted animal is restored to its mother and I'm stuck with you for two days.' He seized her by the arm and propelled her forcefully up the hill.

'Mr Stanhope – Mark – I really do have to get to the cottage somehow. Jenny may need me.'

He slowed at her more appeasing tone. 'Jenny will have Peter at home with her.'

He quickened his pace again and, scurrying over the rough terrain after him, rain driving in her face, Claudia found it impossible to pursue the argument. When they reached the house he bundled her inside and surveyed her bedraggled figure, a suspicious twitch at the corner of his mouth.

'Give me your jacket and boots and go up to the bathroom. Second door on the left at the top of the stairs. I'll leave a dressing-gown and sweater outside. I don't think I can do anything about the pants.'

Mutely Claudia took off her jacket, then, supporting herself on Mark's shoulder, dragged off her muddy boots. She peeled off her wet socks and tucked them inside the boots. Still without a word, she crossed the hall and mounted the wide staircase.

The bathroom was large, old-fashioned, and rather spartan, but the tub was deep, the water ran hot and there were thick towels. Claudia took off her sweater and damp cords. She washed at the bowl, then, sitting on the edge of the bathtub, soaked her chilly feet in the hot soapy water. She was still wriggling her toes indulgently when Mark tapped on the door.

'Are you all right?'

'Yes.'

'I'm leaving the dressing-gown. There's some coffee when you're ready for it.'

'Thank you. And a brush or comb, please.'

She heard his footsteps retreat along the corridor. She leant back on her perch to inspect her image in the mirror above the wash-basin. Her hair was a wild tawny mane about her shoulders. Her face was, at least, clean, although naked-looking. No make-up, she realized with a jolt. No handbag – perhaps for a couple of days. So, no diary, notebook, pen, not even a handkerchief, to say nothing of a toothbrush or change of underwear. She felt suddenly bereft and vulnerable.

She let out the bathwater and dried her feet. As she put on her sweater which was still dry, she heard Mark return and leave again. Cautiously she opened the bathroom door. On the floor outside lay a black towelling bathrobe, on top of it a hairbrush, a new toothbrush, a pocket-handkerchief and a new pair of woollen socks.

Grudgingly Claudia acknowledged his thoughtfulness as she put on the robe and the socks. She turned back to the mirror and dragged the brush through her hair, pushing it into damp waves framing her face. She left the brush with the toothbrush on a shelf below the mirror, picked up her trousers and went downstairs.

She found Mark waiting for her in a small room near the kitchen that had once perhaps been a housekeeper's room. He indicated a chair drawn up before an electric fire.

'Sit down and warm your toes. I'll get the coffee.'

'Thank you.' Claudia held out her trousers. 'I don't know what to do with these.'

'There's a pulley thing in the kitchen. They'll dry off on that.'

He took the trousers from her and went into the kitchen. Claudia looked around her. There was little furniture in the room – a couple of fireside chairs, a lamp table, a bookcase – but it had a comfortable lived-in look.

'I spend a lot of my time in here,' Mark said, returning. He put a cup of coffee down beside her. 'It saves heating and cleaning in the rest of the house.'

'Yes, I hear you don't like having anyone coming in to clean.'

'I didn't like my last experience. That lady spent most of her time prying. I suppose I should get somebody else. And if you're about to suggest Jenny,' he added, 'she'll soon have more than enough to do.'

'I wasn't going to suggest Jenny. But I still think the Liddells could be useful here. There's masses of work for Peter and Jenny could probably do a little secretarial work even after the baby arrives.'

'I'm not running a creche! Don't you ever stop trying to arrange people's lives?'

She glared at him. 'Don't you *care* about people's lives?'

'Not particularly. And, even less, do I like them taking an interest in mine.'

Claudia drank some of her coffee. She said coldly, 'I should phone Jenny. She'll be worrying about me.'

'Surely not. Peter saw what happened. But phone her, by all means, if you want to.'

'Thank you. I should be there with her; she isn't well.'

'Don't worry, they won't be cut off. If anything goes wrong Peter can get her to the doctor.'

'But there are the children—'

'I'm sure Peter can manage.' Mark's tone was growing impatient. 'I'm sure he's a regular New Man – caring, sensitive, sharing the family responsibilities.'

'As a matter of fact, he is.'

'But still with that essential masculinity!' He slammed down his coffee cup and crossed to the window, looking out at the dripping vegetation. With his back turned from Claudia, he said, 'Was it a good idea, your coming here?'

She stared. 'You practically *dragged* me here!'

'I'm not talking about coming to my house. I mean coming here at all. Staying with the Liddells. Why don't you leave them alone? It's obvious that Peter is crazy about you. You may despise their dull little family set-up, but no doubt it's precious to Jenny—'

'How dare you!' To her dismay Claudia found she was shaking with shock and anger. 'And you have the nerve to lecture *me* about prying into other people's business!'

He turned and regarded her bleakly. 'Do you deny that you and Peter were lovers?'

'It's nothing to do with you, but – yes, I do deny it. And I don't despise their family life—' She became aware that, in her agitation, Mark's bathrobe had fallen aside exposing her long, slim legs. She jerked it closed. 'You don't know how much I have envied that life,' she said bitterly.

'So, why are you here? Do you get your kicks seeing Peter jump through hoops?'

Claudia got swiftly to her feet and crossed to the door where she paused. 'I'm here because Jenny appealed to me to come. And her distress is largely caused because she's afraid you're coming to throw them out of their home. So don't preach to me about protecting the family!'

She flung open the door. 'I'll find somewhere else to wait until the river goes down!'

'Please don't flounce out on me. I really can't do with you flouncing through doors for days.'

'*Days*! There's no way I'll stay here for days. I'll swim across first.'

'Now you're being silly. I'm sorry. I shouldn't have spoken to you like that. It's just that I happen to be fond of Jenny and, believe it or not, I like and respect Peter. It seemed dangerous to me — But forget it. Could we try for a *modus vivendi* while you are here?'

'May I phone Jenny?'

'Use the phone in the study. You know where it is.'

She found her way to the study and sat down at the desk. Her heart was thumping in her throat and her hands trembled. How could he have exposed so casually the secret she had locked in her heart for so many years? Exposed it to judgement, sneered at it, condemned it?

The memory of his words made her feel physically sick, but, after a few moments, she pulled herself together with an effort, reached for the phone and dialled the Liddells' number.

Jenny answered the call. 'Claudia!' she burst out

when she heard Claudia's voice. 'What a horrendous thing to happen! Peter told me—'

'Never mind me. I'm perfectly OK. What about you? Will you be all right?'

'Yes, fine. Peter will be here and I'm feeling better. But how will you cope – alone with Mark?'

'I'm quite sure he has no designs on me. How is the water looking down there?'

'About the same. It isn't getting past the sandbags.'

'Well, it goes without saying, I'll be back as soon as possible.'

Jenny would have talked longer, but Claudia replaced the receiver. She put her head down in her hands and was still sitting there when Mark looked round the door.

'Is everything all right?'

'Yes, the river is no higher.'

'That's good. But I really meant, how are you?'

'I'm fine. Did you think that your disgusting remarks would upset me?'

'Well, I hope that they didn't. So – how about coming out of your lair? Our time together will pass more quickly if it's not spent in stony silence.'

'Anything that makes our time together go quicker!' She got to her feet and stalked to the door.

Mark stood aside and followed her back to the sitting-room. 'I was thinking of getting us some lunch. Of course, it won't be as good as Peter could create, but I'll do my best.' He intercepted her scowl. 'What do you expect me to do? A Canute act? Go and glare at the river until it recedes?'

'You could stop making cheap remarks about Peter.'

'Am I treading on sacred ground – making light of the Great Romance? I'll bet you've never told anyone a word about it, have you? Never laughed at yourself a little? Because, if you talked about it, it might dissipate and you don't want that, do you? You want to hug to your bosom the pure concentrated flame.'

To Claudia's dismay, tears flooded her eyes. 'I can't talk about it.'

'I think you should.'

'Why would you want to hear about it? For a big laugh?'

'I don't particularly want to hear about it. But I think it might be a good idea. I think you're all on perilous ground.'

Claudia looked up at him. His face was serious. He took her gently by the arms and sat her down in the easy chair.

Looking down at her bowed head, he said, 'When did you meet?'

She tried to speak, but her voice was husky. She cleared the throat and started again. 'I've known Jenny since I was fourteen years old. Her parents died and she came to live in the next street with her grandparents. She joined my school and we became very close. We were both only children and she spent a lot of time at my home. We were both good at art.' Claudia smiled faintly. 'We used to alternate in winning the school art prize. When Jenny was seventeen she left to do her foundation year at art school. I'm a few months younger, so I was a year behind. I missed her badly, but we talked on the phone and she came home most weekends.'

She lifted her head and pushed her hair from

her brow. 'Then she stopped coming home so often. Almost from the start I'd heard a lot about this terrific fellow-student. How attractive he was, how talented, how utterly unattainable—'

'Just a minute,' Mark interrupted. 'This was *Peter*?'

'This was Peter,' Claudia said firmly. 'One day, in the spring, Jenny rang me up. She was ecstatic. The young man had asked her to go out with him. After that, I saw even less of her. She couldn't bring him home to the sour old grandparents, so she spent even the vacations at college. The romance seemed to be progressing and I was happy for Jenny. She's had a rough deal up till then.

'I was longing to meet the fabulous Peter, but it didn't happen until I joined them at college in October. And then my reaction was the same as yours – what was the fuss about?'

She smiled again, lost in those faraway times. 'You know Peter – he's no sex object; he's not drop-dead handsome – but I liked him right away. More than liked him – I was strongly attracted to him. He had a quality – God, how could I explain it to you? He had enormous charm – not obvious charm, but a sweetness—'

Her voice faltered and stopped. She twisted the sash of Mark's bathrobe.

'What was his reaction to you?'

'He was attracted. You always know. So I was circumspect. I made my own circle of friends. I didn't see a lot of Jenny and Peter and I never saw Peter alone. I knew I could very easily fall in love with him.'

'Didn't Jenny suspect anything?'

'Our attraction? There was never anything to suspect. No. She has a very trusting nature.'

'That's always such a help.' He caught her angry glance. 'I wasn't getting at you. I was speaking—'

'Not personally, surely? I can't imagine you being very trusting.'

'I wasn't always this way. But, I was going to say, I was speaking generally. Look, how about a break? Shall I rustle us up something to eat?'

Claudia noticed how adroitly he had turned the conversation away from himself. 'That sounds good.'

He led the way to the kitchen where he reached up to the pulley to feel the legs of Claudia's cords. 'Nearly dry. You'll be able to brush the worst of the mud off soon.'

'Good. I wouldn't be unburdening myself to you like this if I had my trousers on!'

To her amazement, he looked confused. He said hurriedly, 'I've got soup and some cold chicken.'

'Can I do anything?'

'You could set the table. We'll eat in here where it's warm. Cutlery in the drawer, plates in the cupboard below it and wine glasses in the next one to it.'

Mark worked swiftly and efficiently, decanting soup from a blender, then slicing tomatoes and pepper for a salad.

Claudia raised her eyebrows. 'Home-made soup?'

'One has to do something in the evenings.'

'What else do you do besides making soup?'

'I read a lot. Call up friends – yes, I do have some. Work on designs.'

He stirred the soup, then fetched a bottle of wine

from the pantry. He set out a wooden platter of bread, then shared the soup between their bowls.

The soup was very good and, after the stress of the morning, Claudia ate with relish. Mark poured the wine and replaced the soup-bowls with plates of sliced chicken and salad.

When they had finished eating and he had made coffee, he said, 'So that's all there ever was between you and Peter? I owe you an apology.'

With a jolt Claudia was brought back to her reminiscence. She drained the last of her wine. 'No, there was a little more than that.' She paused, thinking back. 'I enjoyed my time at college. I loved the work, I had a lot of friends, a few affairs. Then, halfway through my second year, two things happened, unfortunately together. I was sharing a roomy, but expensive, flat and my room-mate decided to quit the course and, in the same week, Jenny's landlady suddenly needed *her* room and asked her to leave.

'Financially, I had to share. What could I do but ask Jenny to move in? She thought it a heaven-sent coincidence. There was no way I could turn her down, although I knew it would mean seeing more of Peter.'

She turned her wineglass stem between her fingers. 'It was then that Peter did his painting of me. You know the one.'

Mark smiled. '*Claudia on the Wing*.'

Claudia flinched. 'Yes. After Jenny moved in, Peter was around all the time. It wasn't easy and we were both constrained. I think Jenny believed we didn't like each other. Anyway, Peter had done several portraits of Jenny and she suggested that he should paint me. We both protested as much as we reasonably could but we finally ran out of excuses. It meant that we had to spend quite a lot of time together, usually alone, and it was then that we realized how much we loved each other.'

Her voice was ragged and she stopped. After a moment, Mark asked, 'What did you do about it?'

'What could we do? We did nothing.'

'I don't believe it!' Mark stared at her. 'You were kids – students. Why didn't Peter break with Jenny then? Why is he still mooning over you years later when he has a pack of children?'

'I couldn't have hurt Jenny. Peter was *hers*. He was the only love she had ever had.'

'No. Merely the first.'

She ignored the interruption. 'And I don't think Peter would either. He loved Jenny, too, in a different way.'

'The best of both worlds – now that's a concept I can understand!'

She didn't rise to his bait. 'I suppose that's how it would appear.'

'So that was the end of it?'

'Quite soon after that Peter and Jenny graduated. Peter got a teaching post in Newcastle and Jenny took a part-time job to be near him.'

She stood up and began to clear the dishes from the table. Mark joined her, putting things away, while she ran hot water into a bowl.

'Six months later they were married,' she said flatly. 'And, twelve months after that, Amy was born. I went to their wedding, of course, but I saw little of them after that. I was working hard in my final year and, later, I was involved in my career. My feelings for Peter faded into the background.'

She lifted the last plate from the water and dried

her hands. Mark dried the plate and hung the teatowel over the pulley. He felt Claudia's trousers again.

'They're dry, if you want to put them on. Do you feel like a stroll?' He pointed through the window. 'The sun's coming out. We could go down to the river and see what the position is.'

Claudia took the trousers from him. 'Do you have a clothes-brush?'

'Put them on. It'll be easier to brush them *in situ*.'

She went out of the kitchen into a small scullery where she slipped on the trousers which were stiff with mud. After a minute, Mark joined her outside and began to wield the brush. Claudia stood still, conscious of his warm hand on her waist. She looked down at his glossy dark head and was suddenly acutely aware of the firm strokes down her legs. Something of her discomfort must have communicated itself to him for he straightened up quickly.

Without looking at her, he said, 'That's more presentable. Now, how about that walk?'

Claudia glanced at the sky where there were now large areas of blue. 'I'd like that. I've been longing for a break in the weather for days.'

'Can you manage without your jacket? It's probably still wet.'

'Yes, I'll be fine.'

Mark fetched her wellington boots and, when she had put them on, led the way across the neglected gravelled area at the rear of the house. They skirted the knoll of trees and reached the crest of the hill where she had walked with Peter. The ground was still very wet and rain dripped from the trees. Once Claudia almost lost her footing and Mark firmly tucked her hand beneath his arm.

When they had gone a short distance, they stopped and looked down the hill. The river still flowed, wide and fast, along its new-found course. The Liddells' cottage resembled a small beleaguered castle at the centre of a great brown moat.

'I felt sure Peter would be keeping a vigil on the bank,' Mark murmured.

Claudia felt able to smile. 'I can't believe I'm here. And I certainly can't believe the way I've been talking to you!'

'It's been an odd sort of a day, all things considered. How often have you leapt into rivers to rescue sheep? How often have I rescued young women – plus sheep – and lured them home with me? Your soul-baring is a well-documented reaction to just such a situation.'

'Will the cottage be safe? It looks dreadfully vulnerable.'

'I was assured it was safe from flooding when I bought it. In any case, even if the water did reach it, the Liddells could get out to the village.'

'What about the other cottages? There are two more, aren't there?'

'Yes, but they're almost derelict. They're on high ground well above the river.'

Claudia looked at the sheep grazing far below them. 'Do you think the sheep will be all right?'

'They will, unless they insist on plunging into the river. I phoned the farmer when you were in the bathroom to tell him what had happened, but he seemed pretty phlegmatic. A regular occurrence, I gather.'

They turned away and continued along the

ridge. The hill below was emerald green, sparkling with raindrops. Claudia shivered slightly in the pure, keen air.

Mark tightened his grip on her hand. 'You're getting cold. We'll go back and have some tea.' He caught her sidelong glance. 'You'll have to come back to the house. It's obviously impossible to get to the cottage.'

She grimaced ruefully. 'I'm resigned to that.'

'Thanks a lot!'

They quickened their pace and, in a few minutes, arrived at two dilapidated, windowless cottages facing down the hill towards a farm that nestled in the bottom of the valley. Attempts had been made to repair the wall round the small gardens and piles of slates lay ready to fill the holes in the gaping roofs.

'Are these the other cottages?' Claudia asked.

'Yes. I don't know why they were allowed to get into such a state. Of course, Brackenfield was never a working farm, so they wouldn't have needed a lot of tied cottages. The one the Liddells are in has been rented for a long time.'

They were on delicate ground. Claudia said, 'It would be a shame to let them fall into ruin. They're in a beautiful position.'

Mark kicked at the wall, dislodging a pile of stones. 'I won't do that.'

They climbed away up the hill from the cottages and were soon at the rear entry to Brackenfield. Mark made at once for the kitchen where he put on the kettle and stood by the stove rubbing his hands. 'It's really chilly. I long for the spring – it's been a hellish winter.'

Claudia took off her boots and joined him at the

stove. It hadn't, in fact, been a particularly hard winter. It had been almost mild. Did it seem harsh to him compared with southern winters? His face told her nothing, but she suspected he had not been speaking of the weather.

The kettle boiled and she made tea, bringing the mugs to the stove.

'Thanks. Biscuits in the tin if you want them.'

'Not for me.'

'We'd better see about a bed for you. I don't know what you'll sleep in.'

'I'll manage.'

There was an awkward silence. To break it, Claudia said, 'I should try to get some work done. I've fallen badly behind. I had intended to go home for a few days.'

'Is it anything you can do here?'

'Well, there is my newspaper article. I'm right up against my deadline.'

'You write for the papers?'

Claudia smiled at the distaste on his face. 'It's one of my sidelines. Don't you care for journalists?'

'I detest them.'

She considered telling him that the article in question was a feature on 'Lightweight Summer Knits', but his rudeness decided her against it. 'I may make a few preliminary notes – if it won't offend your sensibilities.'

'Not at all. I'll sort out a room for you.'

He put down his mug and led the way upstairs. A large window on the landing provided a fine view of the gentle, sloping pasture at the back of the house. Turning down the passage, Mark opened a door opposite the bathroom.

'I've only furnished a couple of bedrooms, but

this one is quite pleasant.' He stood aside, then followed Claudia into the room.

It was a big room. The faded blue-sprigged wallpaper probably dated from Mrs Cunningham's day, but had been matched by a deep-blue carpet and a blue-flowered duvet. The light wood furniture looked expensive and almost new.

Mark looked about him. 'There's an electric blanket on the bed. The bathroom, you know, is right across the corridor. I'll bring you some towels. Is there anything else you need? Paper, pens? I wouldn't want to hold up the flow of creation.'

'No, thanks. I think I'll lie down for a while. Perhaps I can think up an angle.'

That got no reaction and he turned and left the room.

A small electric fire had been fitted into the fireplace and Claudia switched it on. Despite an initial stench of burning dust it crackled into a welcome glow and Claudia stretched her cold fingers to it. She looked in the mirror above the fireplace. She looked frightful, her unmade-up face was pale, her hair dishevelled, her trousers filthy.

She took off the trousers and her sweater and lay down on the bed, pulling the duvet over her. It wasn't so much that she was physically tired, but her nerves and emotions felt as taut as a bowstring. What had earlier seemed such an easy intimacy with Mark, now seemed quite incredible. How could she have confided in him things that no one else had ever got from her?

He was a dangerously attractive man and it would be very easy to repeat her mistake. To fall for another married man. To throw away more years of her life. There was something suspect about him, too. His flight to this remote place, his mistrust of intruders, his dislike of journalists.

A scurry of raindrops hit the window. The sky had darkened. The fire spread its comforting warmth. Claudia sighed and snuggled beneath the cover. Tomorrow she would get back to the cottage somehow and then she would return home, safe from disturbing emotions. Home to her work, her flat, her independence. That was what she would do, she decided as her eyelids drooped. She would write herself out of the script.

Six

Claudia was awakened by a tap at the door. She sat up, struggling for a moment to recall where she was. Then her situation rushed in on her. She had been asleep in Mark Stanhope's bed. In one of Mark Stanhope's bedrooms, she corrected hastily. And she had dreamt. The dream flooded back more vivid than reality. She had been posing for her portrait again, but, this time, behind the wing chair she was naked and the artist looking at her with such intensity was not Peter, but Mark.

The knock came again. Involuntarily, Claudia glanced down. She was decently covered by the T-shirt she had worn beneath her sweater. She attempted to smooth her tousled hair and called, 'Come in.'

Mark looked round the door, a couple of towels over his arm. 'I was wondering what had become of you.'

'I'm sorry, I fell asleep. What time is it?'

'Nearly six.'

'Good heavens! I switched on the fire and it got so warm—'

'No harm done.' Mark turned off the fire in the now very warm room. 'Although I suppose you didn't get anything done on your article.'

'No. The world will have to wait a little longer for the latest word on summer knitwear.'

His face broke in a shamefaced smile. 'Is that your subject?'

'That's it.' She grinned. 'Did you expect an exposé of your mysterious past? You look too young to be Lord Lucan and if you're Shergar the plastic surgery is terrific!'

He snatched up a pillow and sideswiped her with it. 'I just happen to have an instinctive dislike of the Press. I have steaks waiting downstairs – are you interested?'

'Passionately. Could I bathe first?'

'Certainly.' He withdrew and Claudia put on the bathrobe, picked up the towels and made for the bathroom. She filled the tub and relaxed in a long soak. The sleep and the bath restored her composure. Fresh clothes would have been nice, but there was nothing she could do about that, so she towelled briskly, got back into her sweater and trousers and gave her hair a strenuous brushing.

It was almost dark when she went downstairs, the landing window framing a pewter-grey sky shot through with streaks of pearly-pink.

She found Mark in the kitchen. 'At least the body is clean, if the apparel leaves something to be desired. Can I do anything to help?'

'Everything is under control. Potatoes baking, salad made, the wine breathing.'

'How insufferably efficient. Can I set the table?'

'Already done. We're going to be civilized and eat in the dining-room.'

Claudia left him and wandered along to the dining-room. It was a large well-proportioned room with two big sash windows and an elaborately carved plaster ceiling. The walls and carpet were rose-red and deeper red curtains covered the windows. Two places were set at one end of the polished table.

In a few minutes Mark nudged open the door carrying a large tray. He speedily transferred the plates and dishes to the table and filled their glasses.

He raised his glass to Claudia. 'Will you propose a toast?'

She raised her own glass. 'Here's to the flood abating.'

He scowled in mock disgust. 'I call that downright unsociable!'

She sipped her wine. 'You've been very hospitable, but you know that's what I want.'

'I phoned the cottage while you were bathing.'

'Are they all right?'

'Fine. Still cut off from us, though.'

'If the river's no lower by tomorrow, I'll try to find another way round by the road.'

'You certainly do a lot for a fellow's ego! I lend you my socks, I ply you with steaks—'

'I said I was grateful. But playing desert island is not what I'm here for.'

'You take your duty very conscientiously, but Peter is there and, as we agree, he's the business.'

Claudia looked at him sharply, but he was chewing his steak innocently.

'How's the steak?'

'Very good.' So was the rest of the meal, and the wine, and Claudia began to enjoy herself. Mark was in an outgoing mood. He talked of the boatyard that his father had built forty years before, the boats on the stocks, sailing trips he had made. It seemed to Claudia that he hadn't talked personally at any length for a long time. She responded by telling him of facets of her work and her own beginner's attempts at sailing.

They sat for a long time over the meal, Mark refilling their glasses. Claudia was aware of a growing intimacy between them and, despite strong misgivings, her attraction to him. Nor was it possible to be unaware that it was returned.

There was just one jarring moment in their conversation. Mark had referred to a costly error of judgement made by his manager. Claudia said, 'I understood you had a very good manager.'

'I do now. This was his predecessor.'

'You got rid of him?'

'Not literally.' He smiled mirthlessly. 'He died, but there was no connection. It wasn't cause and effect.'

Sensing the break in the atmosphere, Mark began to pile their dishes on to the tray. 'Would you like some icecream – or cheese?'

'Nothing for me.'

'I'll get the coffee, then. We'll have it in the sitting-room.'

She helped him to carry the dishes through to the kitchen where they stacked them on the draining-board. When the coffee had perked, Mark led the way to the sitting-room, another large, attractive room, its soft furnishings mainly silvery-blue and with some fine antique pieces, but Claudia was chiefly conscious of the huge sofa in front of the fireplace. While she looked round hastily for a chair, Mark put the coffee tray down on the sofa table and lit the electric fire. He gestured at the sofa and Claudia huddled at the extreme end of it.

With a faint smile he took the other end, passing

her a cup of coffee. 'Can you hear me from there, or shall I use semaphore?'

Claudia made a show of relaxing, moved a full three inches nearer the centre and accepted her cup.

'How long do you expect to stay at the cottage?'

'I really don't know. As long as Jenny needs me. But I shall have to go home for a couple of days soon. I have some engagements and work is piling up.'

'I'll see that Peter is free to take the children to and from school.'

'Thank you. They haven't wanted to try your forbearance too far.'

'The hardhearted landlord?' He grimaced. 'The Liddells are fortunate to have you to call on.'

'They're old friends.'

'And perhaps, there is a little guilt, too?' He raised an eyebrow at her. 'Although I don't know why there should be. You and Peter seem to have behaved impeccably. You didn't do anything about your feelings for each other. You never even declared yourselves.'

There was a long pause, then Claudia sighed. 'Wrong on both counts. I didn't feel guilty – I felt that I had made the sacrifice – and we did declare ourselves. We were lovers.'

She sensed his immediate withdrawal. His understanding changed to the cold demeanour of their first meetings. 'I see. You hadn't finished your story.'

She set down her cup. 'It was only once,' she said, 'but Peter was married by then and Amy born. My parents were living in Newcastle at the time – quite near Jenny and Peter. One morning I had a phone call from my mother. My mother, you must understand, is a very strong lady, but she was completely distraught. My father, who was only in his early fifties and apparently perfectly fit, had had a massive heart attack.'

Claudia stole a glance at Mark. Displaying no obvious reaction, he refilled her cup.

'I was in Leeds at the time,' she went on. 'I called my office and drove straight to the hospital in Newcastle. He was in intensive care. He hung on for forty-eight hours and my mother and I never left him. When he died, I took her home and helped to make arrangements. Then I had to go back to work before returning for the funeral. My mother insisted on it. It was a new job and I was in the middle of my first presentation.'

She sipped her coffee, her eyes full of pain as she relived that faraway time. 'I had made a huge effort not to break down. To be strong for my mother. But I had adored my father and, as I drove off that morning and was within a half-mile of Jenny's home, I just wanted to throw myself in her arms and bawl.

'I thought it was safe to call. It was mid-morning, Peter would be at school. I knocked at the door and – you can guess the rest. Peter was at home – it was half-term – and Jenny was out, visiting friends on the other side of the city. He closed the door behind me, I started to cry and he took me in his arms.' Her voice shook. 'We crammed three years into the next two hours, then I left. I didn't see either of them again until last week.'

Mark said slowly, 'I'm sorry. I've misjudged you—'

'What right had you to judge me at all?'

'None whatever. That was arrogant of me. My only concern was that you might destroy the Liddells' marriage and that's not my business, either. Did you ever have any regrets?'

'Neither of us could have hurt Jenny. That was out of the question. What could we have done?'

'I don't know,' he said slowly, 'but I don't think I could have let you go.'

There was an awkward silence. Claudia felt the blood rush to her cheeks. When she found her voice, she said, 'Well, it's history now and I'm glad we acted as we did.' In an attempt to lighten the atmosphere, she said, 'Shouldn't we do the dishes?'

'Oh Claudia!' He laughed, which somehow had the effect of propelling him some way along the sofa towards her. He caught a tendril of her hair and twisted it round his finger. 'Don't put the drawbridge up again!'

He moved closer and drew her towards him, his arm encircling her waist. Claudia's eyes met his for a moment with something like panic, then his head came down and his lips were on hers, at first gently, rapidly becoming hard and questing. Her arms stole around his neck and, her senses reeling, she found herself matching his hunger. His kisses roused her more than any she had ever experienced, seeming to melt her very bones until she fused against his body.

Her pliancy inflamed him. His breath was harsh and rapid and his hand thrust beneath her sweater with trembling urgency to cup her breast. He groaned with desire and Claudia began to feel herself lost to him. She slid lower on to the sofa. Then, piercing the moment, the doorbell shrilled through the house.

Mark raised his head with a furious oath. His eyes were hot with unslaked desire, his hair tumbled over his brow. Claudia stared at him, stunned. The doorbell shrilled again. He stood up, pushed the hair from his forehead and strode across the room, savagely wrenching the door wide. Claudia followed him, reaching the hall just as he opened the front door. The light from the hall fell on to Peter outlined in the doorway.

He seemed to quail before Mark's expression. 'Oh, hi, Mark. We wondered whether you realized that the water had gone down.'

Claudia joined Mark at the door. At a loss for words, she repeated feebly, 'The water has gone down?'

Peter looked from one to the other of them. 'It's been down for hours.'

'Oh, that's – wonderful.' Claudia looked doubtfully at Mark who had stood aside, an inscrutable expression on his face. 'I'll get my things.'

She shot off to the kitchen where she scrambled into her jacket and boots. When she got back to the front door the two men didn't appear to have spoken.

She smiled at Mark. 'Thank you for looking after me so well. I'm sorry about the washing-up.'

'Think nothing of it. It will help to pass the evening.'

'It was very kind of you. I'll get your socks back to you.'

Mark smiled thinly at them, stood aside and closed the door.

Peter tucked Claudia's arm beneath his own. 'You must be relieved that's over,' he said, a faint note of query in his voice. 'I'd have come sooner, but the kids were too excited by events to settle down.'

'What time is it?'

'Nearly nine.'

'And we can really get through?'

'It's pretty mucky, but about five, the river suddenly turned and poured back into its old channel.'

Claudia stopped. 'What time?'

'Around five o'clock.'

'But when Mark phoned the cottage you said you were still cut off.'

'Mark never phoned.'

'Perhaps he spoke to Jenny—'

'There was no phone call.'

'But Mark said—'

'I don't care what Mark said. He didn't phone.' Peter's voice was querulous. 'He lied to keep you at the house all night. Did he come on to you?'

'Of course not.' It was shading the truth, but 'coming on to' was altogether too one-sided for what had just been taking place.

A wave of irritation washed over her – at Peter's sullen face, at Mark's cheap deception; most of all, for her own whole-hearted response to his sexual overture. More than ever she was resolved to escape from Brackenfield.

They plodded on in silence through the mud. When they reached the cottage Jenny came out to meet them while Claudia struggled out of her boots.

'Oh, Claudia, thank heaven you're back. Was it absolutely ghastly?'

Claudia took off her coat. 'Well, it wasn't the shortest twelve hours of my life.'

'How on earth did you pass the time?'

'In bed for a good part of it.' As Peter's head

jerked round, she added, 'It kept me out of Stanhope's way.'

'But why didn't you come back earlier?'

'She didn't come back because Mark told her we were still cut off.'

'Oh-ho!' Jenny grinned.

The innuendo soured Claudia's mood further. 'In fact, he was perfectly courteous. It was just embarrassing.'

'I'm sorry—'

'It wasn't your fault. I acted like an idiot. Can we go in? I'm freezing.'

'Oh, of course. I'm sorry,' Jenny said again. She glanced at Claudia, unused to brusqueness in her.

The three of them went into the living-room where a fire glowed in the hearth. Claudia went over and crouched beside it. 'My clothes are filthy; I must change.'

'I saved you some supper,' Jenny said. 'Shall I warm it up?'

'No, thanks, I have eaten. I think I'll go to bed shortly.'

'A drink, then?' Peter said.

'I've had a lot of wine, but perhaps a small whisky.'

Peter poured their drinks. Claudia sipped her whisky, its warmth relaxing her. She smiled. 'It's good to be back.'

Jenny said timidly, 'So he wined and dined you?'

'And lunched me. All cooked with his own fair hands. After lunch we went for a walk – he showed me the other cottages – then I pleaded exhaustion and took to my bed.'

She wasn't to be allowed to get away with that. 'What did you talk about?'

'Oh, you know, just generalities.' She put down her empty glass. 'By the way, would you two mind if I went home for a couple of days? There are some things I must do and I really must collect some clean clothes.'

'Go whenever you like,' Peter exclaimed. 'It's been incredibly good of you to have done as much as you have.'

'I'll be back – if you wan't me, that is.'

'Well, of course, we want you,' Jenny said. 'It's been great having you here. And I'm sorry about the fiasco today.'

'I'll put it down to experience. Anyway, if you feel poorly give me a ring and I'll drop everything and whizz back.'

With that out of the way, Claudia settled down to listen to the Liddells' account of their day in their island fortress. The children had been highly excited by the experience, but, despite Ben's best efforts to heave the sandbags aside, the ramparts had held.

Peter went out to make them hot drinks and soon it was eleven o' clock.

Claudia yawned. 'And I was going to have an early night.'

She said goodnight and went upstairs, quickly showered and packed her suitcase, rolling up her muddy trousers and stuffing them into a corner.

She climbed into bed and lay back against the pillows, happy at the prospect of a few days' break away from Brackenfield. It seemed to her that she now had two problems instead of one. What would have happened between her and Mark if Peter had not arrived on the scene? Would Mark have been with her now?

No, of course, he wouldn't, she assured herself firmly. She was not in the habit of going to bed with new acquaintances. And yet, remembering the way her body had melted in his arms, she knew that she couldn't have trusted her response. And, hours later, as she lay restless in the darkness, her treacherous body yearned for his caresses.

She woke early the next morning to find the sun shining through the curtains. She went quickly to the window and was relieved to see the river still in its old route, though running fast and wide. She used the bathroom, then dressed quietly, only going downstairs when she heard someone moving below.

It was Jenny. 'I was going to bring your breakfast in bed on your last morning.'

Claudia sat down at the table. 'How are you feeling?'

'I'm fine.'

'You promise to phone if you need me?'

'I promise.' Jenny set two plates on the table and started to scramble some eggs. 'If you promise not to get marooned at Brackenfield next time.'

'I promise, I promise!' Claudia grinned. 'But you should have seen me with that sheep, Jen!'

Jenny made tea and toast and brought it to the table with the eggs. As they were finishing, Peter, Ben and Amy came downstairs. The children were tearful to hear that Claudia was leaving and only appeased when she promised to return soon with more story books. After lengthy goodbyes, Peter carried Claudia's suitcase to the car.

He put the case in the boot and leant in at the window. 'Thanks for everything, Claudia. It's been wonderful seeing you again.' He hesitated. 'You're

not going because of anything Mark said – or did –
are you?'

'Of course not. But he doesn't seem such an
ogre, Peter.'

'He did lie to you about not being able to leave –
but I guess that's not hard to understand.' He bent
to kiss her. 'Come back soon, Claudia.'

She put the car into gear and drove carefully
along the muddy track to the gates. She glanced up
the hill towards the house but there was no sign of
life and she turned between the gateposts into the
lane. As she turned off the lane for the road to
Otterburn, the strain of the past week seemed to
fall from her shoulders.

She enjoyed the drive. The day was crisp and
bright and when, at mid-morning, Durham's
spectacular skyline came in view she was in good
spirits. She negotiated the narrow streets to her
house, got her case from the car and carried it
upstairs.

Claudia switched on the answerphone. There
were half-a-dozen non-urgent calls. The last call,
made that morning by her mother, told her that
the mail and phone calls had not seemed
sufficiently important to forward and, if she hadn't
heard from Claudia before, she would phone the
cottage at six o'clock.

There was a small pile of letters beside the
phone. Claudia picked them up and skimmed
through them. Her mother was right, there was
nothing of importance. She put on some coffee
while she unpacked her case.

When the coffee was ready she carried it
through to her workroom where she trawled
through the work-in-progress, happy to pick up

the threads of her normal life again. There was, as always, a sketch-pad on the table and, pulling it to her, she began to doodle idly. Soon forceful strokes filled the page. Portraiture was not her usual forte, but in the arrogant line of the nose, the quizzical eyebrow, the long, firm mouth, Mark Stanhope was unmistakable. Claudia tore off the sheet, crumpled it and tossed it in the wastebin, irritated that his disturbing presence should invade her sanctuary.

She loaded the washing machine, did some housecleaning and watered her plants. Then she made a sandwich and returned to the workroom where, this time, she succeeded in immersing herself in some half-completed jobs.

At five o'clock she made a pot of tea, settled on to the settee and dialled her mother's number.

In a moment her mother picked up. 'Hello, darling. Good to hear from you. Are you still with Jenny?'

'No, I got back this morning.'

'How is she?'

'OK at the moment, but she varies from day to day. The problem is that she's pregnant and they're afraid she'll lose the baby. I've been helping out and looking after the children. I'll probably go back again.'

'Poor Jenny. Peter must be worried about her while he's out at school all day.'

'Peter isn't teaching now, so he's around a lot of the time.'

'So how are they living?'

'Well – that's another problem.' Claudia described the situation at Brackenfield. 'They seemed to have been happy with the life. The cottage is very pleasant, but it's tied and now the new owner is being difficult and wants possession.'

'But does he know their circumstances?'

'He didn't buy the property with a sitting tenant. I suppose one can see his point of view—'

'I can't,' Claudia's mother said sharply. 'It sounds very callous.'

'Yes, you're right, of course. They're hoping he'll change his mind. Finding somewhere to live with three young children and – I imagine – very little capital won't be easy.'

'And work for Peter, too. I can't understand why he gave up teaching.'

Close as she was to her mother, Claudia had never been able to discuss Peter with her. Firmly she moved the conversation away from Brackenfield before ringing off.

She was in the kitchen wondering what she might prepare for her evening meal when there was a knock at the door. She opened it to find Paul Werner outside.

'Ah, Claudia, I am glad that you are back. Maria and I, we like to know that you are upstairs.'

Claudia smiled at him. 'I may have to go away again for a short time. I'm looking after a sick friend.'

'Then will you have supper with us tonight? We should be so happy to have your company.'

Claudia's heart sank. She felt that she had been too much in company for the past few days and she longed for some time on her own, but, confronted with her old neighbour's beaming face, she melted. 'Thank you, Paul. I'd like that very much.'

They settled on seven o'clock. Claudia tidied away her work, ironed her laundry, showered and

changed into the sort of pretty, feminine attire of
which the Werners approved.

She went downstairs to the ground-floor flat.
Maria Werner greeted her warmly and ushered
her into the sitting-room. In the northern English
city the Werners had created a little of the charm of
old Vienna. All was red velvet and gilt and mirrors,
with Meissen figurines poised on every surface.
Claudia sat on the enveloping settee and accepted a
glass of wine.

Maria was an excellent cook with total disregard
for the latest pronouncements on healthy eating.
Dietary fibre and low-fat were concepts that had
never entered her vocabulary. Claudia sipped her
wine and regarded the Werners fondly.

Both were short and plump. A halo of fluffy
white hair surrounded Paul's bald head. He wore a
velvet smoking jacket of which his cheroot made
full use. Maria, whose high-piled grey hair still
showed traces of an unlikely gold, was wearing
green panne velvet with several trailing chiffon
scarves. They argued, contradicted, laughed and
supported each other. Claudia thought it a
wonderful marriage.

This evening a delicious chicken dish was
followed by a cream-smothered strudel, excellent
coffee, brandy and much talk. The Werners
tended to repeat their anecdotes, but their
conversation was so lively and their accents so
charming that Claudia invariably enjoyed an
evening in their company. At eleven o'clock she tore
herself away leaving them still in sparkling form.

She fell asleep quickly and, when she woke, it was
as if the previous evening had acted as a firebreak
between Brackenfield and the present. Almost

seamlessly she slid back into her routine of work, talking to colleagues and instigating new projects. For three days she pushed Brackenfield successfully to the back of her mind. She no longer thought of Peter with the old pain, but with a faint, sweet emotion akin to nostalgia. She didn't allow herself to think about Mark at all.

On the fourth morning she woke early to bright sunshine. She put on a tracksuit and running shoes, tied back her hair, and let herself quietly out of the house. She jogged evenly through the narrow streets towards the city centre. Soon spring would bring the hordes of visitors, but, this morning, she could still run unimpeded. She reached Framwellgate and dropped down to the riverside where she picked up her stride. Beside the path the heavily wooded banks rose steeply. Across the Wear the Norman castle and the great cathedral loomed dramatically.

When she reached Prebends' Bridge she stopped and looked back downstream towards the cathedral, her arms resting on the parapet. Below the bridge two racing skiffs skimmed the water like dragonflies, their delicate hulls seeming inadequate to support the hefty oarsmen. She hadn't been out running for months and her blood and pulse thumped heartily.

She crossed the bridge and turned back in the direction she had come, passing below the cathedral's Galilee Chapel. She didn't break stride again until she was home.

At the flat, she showered, then wrapped in her bathrobe, made herself coffee and toast. She was about to start on breakfast when the phone rang. Some instinct told her it was Jenny before she picked up the receiver.

She was right. It was Jenny, almost inarticulate through her tears. 'He's done it, Claudia, just as he threatened. He's put the cottage up for sale!'

Seven

Claudia said, 'Jenny? What are you talking about?'

'I've just told you. Mark has put the cottage on the market.'

'How do you know?'

'Peter overheard him on the phone to the estate agent, yesterday afternoon. He didn't tell me until this morning. I suppose he didn't want me lying awake all night.'

'Did Peter say anything to Mark? Did he tackle him about it?'

'Oh, no. He wasn't supposed to hear the call.'

'Is Peter there now?'

'No, he's taking the children to school. Then he'll go on to work.'

Claudia looked longingly at the coffee cooling on the dining-table. It was still only 9.30 and she didn't feel ready to deal with this. 'What can I do?'

'I know you can't do anything. I just had to talk to someone.'

'Would it help if I came back?'

There was a pause. Claudia thought she heard a sniffle. 'Would you? It's so much to ask.'

'No, it isn't.' Claudia's eyes ranged round her living-room – calm and reassuring, insulating her from upsetting emotions. 'I'd need a little time to tidy up some loose ends.'

'Oh, Claudia, could you—'

'I can probably make it tomorrow. Around teatime again?'

'That would be wonderful. At least you can keep some of the fall-out away from the children.'

'Yes,' Claudia agreed doubtfully. 'Apart from this, how are you?'

'I'm OK.'

They said goodbye. Claudia put down the receiver and returned to the table. The cold coffee and toast looked as uninviting as the next few days promised to be. She ditched the toast in the pedal bin and made some fresh coffee.

What was she expected to do at Brackenfield? She could certainly look after Amy and Ben, but she suspected that Jenny had a hidden scenario. Jenny had half-convinced herself that Claudia had acquired some influence with Mark and could use it on her Liddells' behalf.

She sipped her coffee looking out over the rooftops from the kitchen window. She felt queasy at the thought of confronting Mark. It was true that they had reached a sort of alliance – her cheeks grew hot at the memory of their last meeting – but she knew he wouldn't be moved over the Liddells and her intercession would only make him more obstinate. It might be best to simply keep out of his way. Yet, recalling those minutes in his arms when she had felt so vibrantly alive, she experienced a pang of regret at the decision.

She dressed and managed to detach herself sufficiently from her worries to get through a number of jobs, breaking off for a lunchtime snack. In the afternoon she made a couple of calls in the city, then decided to visit her mother.

Helen James lived in a neat semi-detached house that she had bought when she obtained her teaching post in the city. Her car was standing in the drive, so Claudia parked at the kerb before walking past the well-kept lawns and borders to the front door.

Her mother had seen her arrival and opened the door. 'Hello, darling. I wondered when I should see you.'

Claudia kissed her. 'Sorry, Mum. I'd got so far behind with things.'

'Have you caught up now?'

'More or less.'

She followed her mother through to the kitchen. Mrs James had just got in from school and was still wearing a trim blouse and skirt. A bulging briefcase had been dropped on the kitchen table.

'Not too early for a sherry, is it?' Without waiting for a reply she got out the bottle and filled two glasses. She kicked off her high-heeled pumps and sunk on to a chair. 'I swear I'm getting too old to cope with those little fiends.'

Claudia looked at her mother anxiously. She was still a good-looking woman with fine features and clear grey eyes. She did look tired, but Claudia knew that she loved her work and would be ready for action again by the morning.

'Don't overdo things. I'll come over and give you a hand with the garden.'

'No, you won't! You don't know the first thing about gardening. Anyway, I enjoy it.'

She sighed deeply, a sigh of relaxation, and flexed her stockinged feet. 'What about you? Have you heard anything from Jenny?'

'She phoned this morning. I said I'd go back tomorrow.'

'Is she poorly again?'

'She's – not very well.'

'Can you tell me what happened to them? Not if it would break a confidence, but, you know, I've always been fond of Jenny.'

Claudia hesitated. Her mother said, 'Are they happy together?'

'Oh, yes, it isn't that.'

'Why did Peter give up teaching? I thought he would make a fine teacher.'

Claudia finished her sherry. As her mother refilled their glasses she told her about Peter's accident and subsequent breakdown and the chain of events that had led to the Liddells' present situation.

'Poor Peter,' Helen James said when Claudia fell silent. 'He was always a sensitive young man. But surely this new owner won't just turn them out?'

'Jenny thinks he will. That's why she was so upset this morning.'

'Don't they have a tenancy agreement? Doesn't Peter have any sort of employment contract?'

'I don't think they've got anything. It's all pretty feudal. They just seem to be there on Mark's forbearance.'

'They should get legal advice. They may have some rights.'

'They're probably afraid of antagonizing him—'

'Antagonizing him! What sort of a man is he? Does he have a family?'

'No, he lives there alone.'

'Why don't you talk to him, Claudia? Perhaps you could—'

'No!' The violence of Claudia's retort bounced off the walls of the kitchen. In a moment she said, 'I've tried to discuss it with him. He's completely unreceptive.'

Helen wiped up the spots of sherry that had leapt from her daughter's glass. She looked at her thoughtfully. 'Is he a young man?'

Claudia drained her glass. She guessed that the 'Mark' she had let slip out had not gone unnoticed. 'He's quite young,' she said shortly. 'Are you going to feed me or not? I'm starving.'

Helen found a chicken pie in the freezer and, while it was heating, she went upstairs to change into a comfortable sweater and slacks. While she was gone, Claudia prepared some vegetables and laid the table. During the meal and for the hour that Claudia stayed after it, they talked of other things. It was only when she was leaving that her mother said, 'Try not to get too upset about Jenny and Peter, and tell them not to worry too much. We can manage something for them in the short term.'

Claudia kissed her mother. 'Thanks, Mum. We'll hope it won't come to that.'

She got home in time to watch a television programme that she wanted to see, then sorted out her packing for Brackenfield.

She was up early next morning. Recalling her promise to take books for the children, she made a quick journey into town to buy a selection, also some food to help with the catering. She had a snack lunch, made some phone calls and, at one o'clock, was on the road.

The route was more familiar now and, sooner than she would have liked, the first sign for Otterburn appeared, followed by the turn for

Marling. As she turned between the gateposts the big, grey house came into view atop the rise. She drove along the track, now drying out, and parked beside the gate. She got out and lifted out her suitcase.

The door to the cottage was ajar. Claudia put her case down in the hall and gave a whistle. A second later two small bodies hurtled into her arms.

'Ouch!' Claudia had subsided to the floor. 'You two are a health hazard!'

'Take it easy, kids!' Jenny smiled at Claudia. 'I really didn't think you'd be back after what we inflicted on you last time.'

'Life was so boring at home. How could it compare?'

Peter came through from the kitchen, a teatowel in his hand. 'Slaving away at the sink, as usual.' He kissed Claudia. 'How are you?'

'I'm fine. How are things here?'

'About the same.' He glanced at the children. 'We'll fill you in later.'

'Claudy, I *missed* you,' Ben announced, his fingers poking enquiringly at her parcels.

'I missed you too, darlings. Now, who's going to help me unpack?'

The children scampered away with their packages while Claudia handed over the food she had brought.

Peter frowned. 'You don't need to do this, Claudia.'

'I know that. But I imagine the village shop is a bit limited.'

'You can say that again!' Jenny inspected the provisions with unmixed pleasure.

Claudia and Jenny watched the children

unwrapping their presents, then joined Peter in the kitchen. He was filling the teapot. Biscuits and a fruitcake were set out on the table.

Jenny cut the cake and handed round cups of tea. 'I feel a bit less panicky now than when I phoned you,' she admitted to Claudia. 'Peter pointed out that the property market is very slow. It could be months before Mark finds a buyer and he'd surely rather have the place occupied than standing empty in the meantime.'

'Yes, that did occur to me,' Claudia agreed, though she didn't think that such an attractive property would take too long to sell. She looked at Peter. 'Has Mark said anything to you directly about selling?'

'Not a word. In fact he has had very little to say at all in the last few days.'

'Not since you left,' Jenny put in without comment.

Claudia hoped desperately that the Liddells would not ask her to intercede with Mark on their behalf. She said awkwardly, 'You know, in the last resort, Mum and I would help—'

To her relief, the children erupted into the room, putting an end to the discussion. They were given their tea and soon it was time for baths and bed. After Claudia, Jenny and Peter had finished their own meal they settled down with drinks in the living-room where they discussed what the Liddells might do if they were forced to leave Brackenfield, each suggestion more outrageous and hilarious than the last, until they retired to bed in almost lighthearted mood.

The next morning Claudia returned to her old routine. She got the children prepared for school

and delivered them, then did what was required
about the house, trying all the time to keep Jenny's
spirits up. She saw nothing of Mark during her
brief excursion outside the cottage. The afternoon
was sunny and she took the children for a walk,
keeping well away from the big house.

The second morning was still sunny. After
dropping the children at school she strolled down
the village street before buying a newspaper and a
bar of chocolate in the sole shop. She drove back to
the cottage and parked by the gate, got out of the
car and slammed the door. As she turned away
Mark Stanhope materialized from the hedge.

Claudia stared. The chocolate slid slowly from its
sleeve to the ground.

Mark bent to retrieve it. 'So, you're back.'

'Obviously.' Claudia strove to steady her heart
which had begun to pound unevenly. 'Where did
you spring from?'

He nodded at a gap in the hedge. 'I often come
down here to gaze at the spot.'

'What spot?'

'The spot where I gathered you up in my arms.'

Claudia flushed. 'I seem to remember it rather as
being dragged.' She put out her hand for the
chocolate.

Mark tossed it lightly between his hands. 'When
did you arrive?'

'Two days ago.'

He raised an eyebrow. 'Have you been avoiding
me?'

'Why should I do that?'

'I've seen nothing of you.'

'There's a lot to do.'

'Let's walk for a little while now. Please,' he

added as she hesitated.

Claudia fell into step beside him, her expression uncompromising.

Mark slipped the chocolate into her jacket pocket. 'I thought we were getting on rather well. Did I offend you that night?'

Claudia felt the blood rush to her face again. 'It would be rather stupid of me to pretend offence, wouldn't it? I seem to recall being fairly responsive.'

'Well, yes, that's how I remember it, but I thought it ungallant to remind you.' He stopped and turned towards her. His face looked older in the thin sunlight. 'What's the matter, Claudia?'

'You know what is the matter.'

'I assure you, I don't.' Then, 'It's not the Liddells and their blasted cottage again, is it?'

'Strangely enough, it is. Your blasted cottage – their home.' Her green eyes blazed. 'You may dislike Peter, but do you have to take it out on Jenny and the children?'

'I don't dislike Peter. Oh, there was a moment when I could have strangled him – I think you know when that was and would agree it was understandable—'

'You must have enjoyed him grovelling to you,' Claudia said bitterly.

'He has never grovelled to me. I wouldn't allow another man to do that.'

She looked away from him. They were at the river's edge near the scene of her rescue. The same cast of sheep gazed at them from across the water.

Mark nodded at one standing a little apart from the rest. 'Do you think that's the one that brought us together?'

She shook her head angrily. 'You won't be serious.'

'Don't you mean I won't do what you want? Will you have lunch with me?'

'I can't.'

'Why not? If you don't trust me at the house we can find a pub.'

'I have too much to do.'

'Dinner, then?'

'Thank you, no.' She turned away. 'I'm going back to the cottage. Jenny will be wondering where I am.'

'Jenny knows where you are. She has been watching us from the bedroom window for the last five minutes, hope shining from her eyes. She thinks you're going to seduce me into letting them have the cottage.'

She looked back at him, her eyes cold with dislike. 'You're disgusting.'

'You could do it, you know!'

She stalked away, her back rigid. When she reached the cottage Jenny was at the bottom of the staircase. 'I see you met Mark.'

Claudia banged the front door behind her. 'Insufferable man!'

'You got on all right when you were stranded up there with him, didn't you?'

'We didn't know then that he'd put the cottage up for sale.'

'Claudia, you didn't tell him you knew about that? Peter was eavesdropping.'

'No, of course not. And he pretended he didn't know why I was – less friendly – towards him.'

'Well – he didn't know.'

'I just feel he's toying with you – with all of us.'

She took off her jacket and went through to the kitchen where she filled the electric jug. 'He asked me to lunch.'

'He did?'

'And dinner.'

'What did you say?'

'No and no.' She perched on the table edge watching the kettle boil.

Jenny got out the coffee mugs. 'Maybe you should go.' At Claudia's mutinous expression, she went on, 'He's an unhappy man, Claudia.'

Claudia filled their mugs. Remembering Mark's final words, she said, 'Do you mean I should – try to get round him?'

'Of course it would be great if he came round to our point of view, but I didn't mean—'

'Seduce him?' Claudia asked bleakly. 'I'm afraid that wouldn't work. He very definitely wasn't born yesterday.'

The two women drank their coffee in silence. Then Claudia patted Jenny's hand. 'Come on, love, things to do! We mustn't let him make us miserable.'

They started on the household tasks, Claudia taking the heavier jobs. As she worked, her meeting with Mark continued to occupy her mind. Should she approach him once more and try to influence him? It seemed a small thing to do.

At 12.15 she left to collect the children from school. When they returned, Peter had come in from work and they sat down to lunch together. The children were in high spirits as usual but, despite their efforts to hide it, it was obvious to Claudia that Jenny and Peter were desperately worried.

When they had finished eating, Peter returned to work and Ben and Amy went upstairs for their rest. Claudia and Jenny washed the dishes together. When they were done, Claudia said causally, 'I think I'll go for a walk. Why don't you put your feet up for a bit?'

Jenny half-met her eyes. 'I think I will.'

Claudia put on her jacket and tied a bright silk scarf at her throat. As she left the cottage behind her, she felt absurdly nervous. She could scarcely march straight up to Brackenfield having so brusquely refused Mark's invitations. She started to amble along the riverbank.

After a while she began to enjoy the walk for its own sake, taking an artist's pleasure in the subtle shading of the hills and the gleaming curve of the river. She had walked for almost half an hour when she reached the derelict cottages. She didn't want to approach any closer to Brackenfield and decided to retrace her footsteps. It didn't appear that she was going to 'accidentally' run into Mark. She would have to try again tomorrow.

She leaned against the dilapidated wall of the cottage and looked over the sweep of the valley and the huddle of farm buildings below.

There was a slight noise of stones sliding behind her. She spun round, her heart leaping. Mark was framed in the open doorway of the nearer cottage.

'For someone with so much to do, you've had a long walk.'

Claudia was momentarily lost for words. not only still startled, but horribly aware of his physical presence so close in this isolated place.

'I wanted to get out for a little while. Everyone else is asleep. Not Peter, of course,' she added hastily.

'Of course.'

He joined her leaning against the wall, but he faced the cottages. He regarded the dismal spectacle ruefully. 'There's a hell of a lot to be done to them and, unfortunately, I'm not much of a hand at this sort of thing.'

She was unlikely to get a better opening. Claudia said, she hoped casually, 'Why don't you let Peter have a go at it? He's probably better than you and you'd be free to do your own work.'

'Oh, I'm sure Peter can do everything better than me!' The words burst from him, leaving him shamefaced. He turned away from her. 'I can't believe I said that—'

It was Claudia's turn to look embarrassed. 'I only meant that it seemed a sensible arrangement.'

'Don't you ever give up?' He nodded at the cottages. 'Do you want to see inside?'

'Is it safe?' His mouth twitched sardonically. 'I mean is the fabric safe?'

'You are safe on both counts.' He stood aside and she slipped through the sagging front door. It led directly into a small, dark living-room, paper hanging from the walls and ceiling. Broken glass and plaster crunched beneath their feet. Behind the living-room a tiny, even darker, kitchen was tucked into the fold of the hillside.

Claudia looked about her. 'M-mm, it's pretty dispiriting, but not hopeless. To make them acceptable nowadays you'd have to destroy their original character, but that really hasn't a lot to recommend it – they're just very basic workmen's cottages. A damp course would be the first essential. The walls are sound. The windows would need to be bigger. They need a lot of plastering, then colourwash – something light and bright.'

She crossed to the boxed-in staircase. 'Open up
the staircase, it loses light and space. It could be
against fire regulations, nowadays, anyway—'

Mark was staring at her. 'You do this sort of
thing?'

'Well, not personally, but I've been involved with
people doing restorations. I've advised on colour
schemes and fabric after the rough work was done.'

She opened the staircase door and climbed the
narrow pitch-dark stairs. At the top were two small
bedrooms and a tiny primitive bathroom. The
front bedroom was bright with sunlight. Claudia
picked her way through the debris to the window.
She looked over the valley. 'The view is glorious.
That makes up for a lot.'

Mark joined her at the window. 'You know,
you're positively inspiring. It could be fun to take
on a project like this – particularly if you would
come in on it.'

'And then you would have three cottages to sell.
You take my breath away! The Liddells are going
to be homeless and you want me to help you with a
"fun" project. That's not what I'm here for – or
had you forgotten?'

'Are you sure you always remember? But this has
nothing to do with the Liddells. You can still cook
and clean, or whatever it is you do for them. I was
merely asking you to advise me on this.'

'I'm sorry I have other things on my mind.'

'Like Peter?' He took hold of her by the
shoulders, looking deep into her eyes. 'Can you
truly say that it's all over between you? I thought
for a moment the other night that you were
beginning to care something for me – until he

arrived to take you away.'

Claudia tried to pull away from him. 'You're being ridiculous. Peter came to escort me to the cottage – where I was supposed to be staying. He was probably sent by Jenny.'

She tried again to break away from him, but he bent his mouth to hers, crushing her protests. Claudia struggled more urgently, knowing that she was letting go, that she was giving herself up to a surge of longing. Only the memory of Jenny's unhappy face gave her the strength to push him away.

'No!' she panted. 'I don't want this!'

He stood back from her, his breath rough and unsteady. 'I was right, wasn't I? Despite all you say, you're still in love with Peter. How can you lecture me about taking Jenny's home when you are taking her husband?'

'That's not true. And – even if it was – you're guilty of exactly what you're accusing Peter of. Or are there different standards for the lord of the manor?'

'What the hell are you talking about?'

'Do you deny that you're a married man?' She rushed on blindly. 'Although, of course, your wife refuses to live with you. I suppose you drove her away with your selfishness and arrogance?'

His dark eyes were as expressionless as stones. 'On the contrary, I indulged her in everything. Perhaps that was my error.'

'I'd like to hear her version of events!'

'I'm afraid that isn't possible. My wife is dead. She was killed in a car crash last winter.'

Eight

There was a dreadful silence. At last Claudia said, 'I'm sorry. God, I'm so sorry.'

'You weren't to know.'

'The people around here think—'

'I don't give a damn what they think. And I certainly don't want their sympathy. It's – not appropriate.'

She didn't want to hear any more. She had her own problems. She had Jenny and Peter's problems. She couldn't deal with a recital of his tragic lost love from Mark.

She said quickly, 'I must go.'

'No, please don't—'

'I'm sorry.' She turned swiftly from the window. As she did so, Mark put out his hand to detain her and, in trying to avoid it, her own left hand jerked against the window. A last shard of glass still embedded in the frame sliced a gash across the side of her hand.

She gave a sharp cry of pain, staring in shock at the blood that filled her palm. Mark snatched a handkerchief from his pocket and folded it around her hand. He said bitterly, 'I can't do anything but hurt you.'

Claudia, her face paper-white, swayed against

him. He put an arm about her shoulders. 'Don't pass out on me. We'll go up to the house.'

'No. I'm all right. I'll go back to the cottage.'

'The house is nearer.' Without another word he led the way down the narrow staircase. When they were outside the cottage he put his arm lightly around her waist as they climbed the hill to Brackenfield.

They went in by the back door. Already Mark's handkerchief was soaked in blood. Claudia leant against the kitchen sink feeling sick. Mark pushed a chair towards her and she sank on to it. He turned on the cold tap.

'Can you hold your hand under that?'

Claudia unpeeled the handkerchief, averting her eyes. 'I'm sorry to be such a baby.'

'My knees are shaking and it isn't my blood.' He left her while he fetched a first-aid box, then peered closely at her hand. 'M-mm, it isn't very deep, although it's quite a big slice. Do you want the village nurse to have a look at it?'

'What do you think? I don't want to bother if it's not necessary.'

'I can dress it for you. Men tend to get cut a lot with tools in the yard, so I've had some experience. I don't think it needs stitching and I can't see any glass.'

'I'll leave it to you, then.' She rested her hand, now leaking only a little watery blood, on a pad of cotton lint. Very quickly Mark drew the edges of the wound together with adhesive strips, wincing as she did. There was a tenderness in him now that, in some strange way, moved her as strongly as his earlier passion. Finally he wrapped her hand in a thick soft bandage.

'How about a drink?'

'A cup of tea would be nice. Then I must—'

He grimaced. 'I know. "Get back to the cottage. They'll be wondering where you are!".'

He cleared away his materials and put on the kettle. When the tea was made he carried the tray through to the sitting-room. Claudia sat down in the corner of the big sofa and took a cup from him.

He said, 'How do you feel? You're very pale.'

'I'm all right. The hand is sore.'

'I'll take you home when you've had your tea.'

She looked down at her hand lying in her lap. 'I'm not much good for anything now.'

'It will soon heal. You can still supervise the children and, if driving is painful, I'll make sure that Peter is free to drive them to school.' He broke off. 'What's the matter?'

Claudia furiously blinked away the tears that had filled her eyes. 'Oh, I don't know where I am with you! One minute you behave like a monster and the next you're – you're kind and thoughtful.'

He sat down on the sofa beside her. 'I know I've behaved impossibly but – it's been a bad year. I just needed to lick my wounds. I didn't want anyone around me.'

He looked at her lying back in the corner of the sofa, her face pale, her green eyes bright with unshed tears. She looked lovelier and more vulnerable than he had ever seen her. He said huskily, 'For that matter, I never know where I am with you. I thought things were going well between us. I even hoped—'

He leant forward and took her teacup, putting it down on the table. 'What happened, Claudia?'

She gave a sniff. After a moment's hesitation, she

said, 'You won't be angry with Peter?'

'I shall very probably be angry with Peter, but go on.'

'Well, Peter overheard you speaking on the phone to an estate agent – putting the cottage up for sale. I know you're perfectly entitled to, but, oh Mark, if you could only see how worried Jenny and Peter are—'

She stopped as his expression cleared.

'Peter is an idiot. He's about as competent an eavesdropper as he is at making up his mind which woman he's in love with. The *cottages*, not the cottage. The ones where you have just come to grief. When I bought the estate I planned to sell the Liddells' cottage in order to renovate this house. It was a matter of economics, I don't have unlimited wealth. But, after you intervened on the Liddells' behalf in such an appealing fashion, I realized what I had half-decided anyway, that I couldn't go through with it. So I decided to see what the other two might fetch.'

There was a pause. Claudia said quietly, 'You didn't tell me.'

'I admit I am arrogant. I just didn't like being pressured – or having Peter rammed down my throat every time we talked.'

'Could I tell them?'

He picked up her bandaged hand and gently kissed each protruding fingertip. 'I suppose that means you're going to dash away again.'

'It means so much to them—'

'I know. Of course, I shall have to get a reasonable sum for the other cottages. I was planning what essential work Peter and I could do on them first when you turned up. When you revealed your expertize, I thought you might help out with some ideas on the interiors.'

'I'd enjoy that.'

'That would be wonderful.' He leant closer and kissed her and Claudia returned the kiss delighting in his mixture of tenderness and passion.

She didn't want to go. She wanted to stay and experience in full the white-hot intensity of feeling that Peter had interrupted previously. Already the throbbing urgency of Mark's body threatened to sweep her along. But the old instinct to run from powerful emotions remained. She had been forced to hide her feelings for too long. This was too fierce, too fast, too capable of hurt.

Very gently she pushed him away from her. 'Mark, I must go.'

His eyes near hers were dark with desire. 'Oh, darling, don't—'

She kissed him softly on the mouth. 'I'll see you again soon.'

He stood up reluctantly, pulling her to her feet. 'I'll get the car out. You still look a bit shaky.'

She followed him outside to the big open shed that served as a garage. She did still feel a little dizzy and was glad not to have to walk back to the cottage. The car did the journey in a couple of minutes, stopping alongside hers at the gate.

Mark opened the car door. He looked at her almost shyly. 'I'll see you soon.'

She nodded, then got out and walked towards the cottage. It looked like a happy ending. A real job for Peter in which he could feel he was earning their accommodation while the restoration of the old cottages would give Mark his alternative source of capital. It was almost too neat to believe. As to

Mark's pursuit of her, she put that to the back of her mind to consider later. She simply couldn't deal with it at the moment.

She opened the door to find Jenny and Peter in the kitchen deciding on the evening meal. They turned as she came in.

Peter said, 'Claudia, are you all right? You've hurt your hand!'

'It's nothing.'

'How did it happen?'

'At the old cottages. I cut it on the window glass.'

He looked at her. 'Who bandaged it?'

'Mark did.' Claudia pulled out a chair and sat down at the kitchen table, suddenly tired.

'You were gone so long,' Jenny said. 'We wondered what had happened to you.'

'I went for a walk and ended up at the cottages. Mark was there. I made rather a fool of myself. I accused him of selling this place and it turned out that it was those cottages that he had put on the market.'

'Oh, thank God!' Jenny exclaimed. 'But you didn't tell him about Peter listening to his phone call, did you?'

'It's all right. He understood.'

'Does that mean we have a stay of execution?' Peter asked.

'Better than that. He isn't going to sell this place at all now. And he wants you to stay on and help him restore the other two.'

They stared at her. 'Are you sure that's what he meant?'

'That's what he said. Yes, I'm pretty sure he meant it.'

'Claudia, you're fantastic! How did you manage

it?' Jenny was laughing and crying at the same time and the strain on Peter's face was dissolving visibly. It should have been a wonderful moment, but, perhaps because of the confusion of her own feelings, the loss of blood, or the soreness of her hand, Claudia felt she was standing outside it.

Hearing the noise, the children rushed in, clambering over Claudia and demanding to see her 'wound'.

Peter shooed them off. 'Claudia, why don't you go up and lie on the bed for an hour? I'll bring you some tea?'

'Thanks, Peter. I think I will.'

She climbed the stairs wearily, surprised at how much the day had taken out of her. She took off her shoes and jeans and lay down beneath the duvet. Jenny, if not Peter, was going to want to know how she had 'managed it' and she wasn't sure how much she wanted to reveal.

Mark's interest in her was obvious but, much as she longed to, she was wary of getting involved. It felt wrong, too, that it should happen under Peter's eyes when their own long attachment was barely dead.

Her train of thought was interrupted by a tap at the door and Peter came in with a cup of tea on a small tray. He set it down on the bedside table and sat down on the foot of the bed.

'Is something the matter?'

'I don't know.' She picked up the cup and drank some tea. 'I'm sorry, Peter, I should be over the moon for you and Jenny, but I seem to be feeling a bit down. Perhaps it's the hand.'

He looked away from her to the window. After a moment, he said, 'Mark has fallen for you, you know. I suppose he told you?'

'Not in so many words, but he made it fairly clear.'

'He fell for my portrait of you.' There was pain in his wry smile. 'Every time he visited the cottage I found him gazing at it. I don't know what I should say to you. I don't really know what kind of a man he is. There's still the little matter of a wife, isn't there?'

'She was killed in a car crash.'

'Good God, is that right? That's terrible. Rumour around the village was that they were separated. Was it recent?'

'Just last winter.'

'Of course, it must have been recent. She was with Mark when they looked over Brackenfield in October.'

'Did you see her?'

'No, Jen and I had taken the kids to Kielder for the day. A couple of people in the village saw them. They said she was very glamorous. Not exactly the type for the Border country. But, why on earth didn't Mark say anything? It would have excused a lot of his behaviour.'

'He doesn't want excuses.'

'Well, it would certainly explain his unhappiness. Perhaps he has turned the corner now with the prospect of working on the old cottages and—' He broke off. 'I can't tell you how grateful we are for your part in this, Claudia.'

'I believe Mark would have come round to this decision without me poking my nose in.'

Peter shook his head dubiously. He picked up the tray. 'I'll leave you to get some rest.' He went downstairs and Claudia lay back, pulling the duvet over her.

Obviously, as Peter had said, the death of his wife

would account for Mark's unhappiness. Yet she felt
his problem was more complex than that. He had
spoken of her sympathy being 'inappropriate'.
Beneath the duvet, a tiny shiver ran through her as
she realized how little she knew of him.

She lay, not sleeping, but drowsily listening to
Jenny's and the children's muted voices. After a
while she got up and took a shower, somewhat
hampered by her bandaged hand. She changed
into a dress and went downstairs where the
children brought their new books for her to read
until bedtime.

Although restrained by the knowledge of the
tragic death of Mark's wife, there was a hint of
celebration in the air. Peter had made a special
meal and produced a bottle of good wine and, as
they dined, Claudia felt able to join in her friends'
pleasure.

They were just finishing dinner when the
telephone rang and Peter went to answer it. He
returned to say that it had been Mark enquiring
about Claudia's hand.

'Poor Mark, alone in that big house.' Jenny was
remorseful. 'We should have asked him to eat with
us.'

'No!' Peter and Claudia exclaimed together.
Their eyes met. Claudia felt too self-conscious to be
with Mark in the Liddells' company. Peter, she
suspected, could not face witnessing the attraction
between them.

'He said not to go in to work until I had taken the
children to school tomorrow,' Peter added.

Claudia's hand got her excused washing-up.
When the others had finished they joined her in
the living-room where they discussed ideas for the

renovation of the two cottages. When Claudia went up to bed she was satisfied that, for the Liddells at least, their troubles were at an end.

She woke the next morning to Peter once more bringing tea to her bedside. She got up, showered and dressed and went downstairs as he was leaving to take the children to school.

'I feel thoroughly spoiled,' she said to Jenny who was starting to prepare breakfast. 'Tea in bed. It's not what I'm here for.'

'Make the most of it. There's a pile of ironing waiting.'

They ate breakfast, then Claudia got out the ironing board while Jenny tidied the kitchen. After about fifteen minutes, Jenny announced from the kitchen, 'Mark is prowling round on the riverbank. Poor soul, he looks so lonely.'

Jenny had absorbed Mark's rapid transition from monster to benefactor with seamless ease. Claudia made no response and, after a minute, Jenny drifted through to the living-room.

'Why don't you go for a walk? It's a lovely morning and you're not doing much good here. You've ironed that dress of Amy's twice already!'

Claudia flushed and folded the dress on to the finished pile. Jenny's face wore the conspiratorial air that she remembered from match-making attempts in their college days.

'I'm not sure that I want to get involved, Jen.'

'Who's talking getting involved? You could just thank him for not selling our cottage.'

'Peter will have done that. I don't have to consolidate it.'

Jenny took the iron from Claudia's hand. 'I don't know what happened between you two, but seeing

him is only going to get harder the longer you put
if off. Unless you plan to avoid him for the entire
time you're here?'

Claudia hesitated. What Jenny had said was true.
She was behaving like a child. She put on her
jacket, scowling at Jenny, and went out by the front
door. She walked down the lane to the gate. As she
went through it she saw Mark cutting through the
hedge fifty yards further up the hill.

There was no doubting his pleasure at seeing her
as he strode down the hill towards her.

Claudia smiled. 'Jenny spotted you from the
window. She wanted me to pass on her thanks
about the cottage.'

'No need for that. Peter thanked me. He's gone
up to the old cottages to get some idea of what we
can tackle ourselves and what we shall need
tradesmen for. I was on my way to join him. I shall
try to look knowledgeable while he explains things
to me.'

'If you're a boatbuilder I hate to think you're so
impractical!'

'Oh, we have buoyancy on our side. Boats don't
fall down.' He looked down at her, his dark hair
lifting in the breeze. 'Do you want to come along,
or have you too much to do?' His eyes were teasing.

'On the contrary, Jenny says I am no use to her
this morning.'

'How is the hand?'

'It's a bit sore and the bandage is awkward.'

They turned up the hill and it was soon obvious
that Mark was making for the house rather than
the cottages.

As they neared it, he said, 'I thought we'd have
some coffee first. I had breakfast early.'

'Fine.' Claudia followed him into the house, through the hall to the kitchen. She took off her jacket and propped herself against the table while Mark busied himself with the coffee. After a minute, his back still to her, he said, 'I'm half surprised to find you still here this morning. I thought you would have taken off.'

'Why should I have done that?'

'You'd got what you came for, hadn't you?'

Claudia walked over to the cooker. she turned off a pan of milk that was on the point of boiling over. 'That wasn't what I came for. I came to help Jenny. I'm very grateful for your decision over the cottage. I hadn't realized there were strings attached.'

'Good God, of course there are no strings attached. What do you take me for? But I would like to see you and I feel you are avoiding me.'

Claudia took over making coffee. She didn't speak until she was pouring it into their mugs. 'I can't honestly completely deny that. I don't think I'm ready to get involved and I don't believe you are. You don't trust people, Mark.'

'We could take it gently. Nothing too serious. You are going to help with the cottages, aren't you?'

'Yes, I'd like that.'

Mark perched on the table, drinking his coffee. Presently he said, 'I'd like to tell you, about Isabel.'

'Your wife?'

'Yes.'

He fell silent, apparently lost in the past. Claudia prompted him gently. 'How long were you married?'

'Two years. She was ten years younger than I, just twenty when we married.'

'When did she – when was the crash?'

'Last October. Ten days after we had looked over Brackenfield.'

He put down his cup and rubbed his hand roughly across his face. 'Isabel's father was a wealthy businessman, a leading figure in the community. I built a boat for him and I got to know Isabel. She didn't have a job and she took to hanging around the yard. She had been spoiled. She was used to getting what she wanted and, apparently, what she wanted right then was me.

'I was flattered, of course. She was very attractive and I knew plenty of other men were keen. I never seemed to have had much time for pursuing women and, almost before I realized what was happening, plans were afoot for the biggest wedding the town had seen for years. I do recall having slightly cold feet. I knew we hadn't a lot in common. Isabel had a very low boredom threshold and she loved to party which wasn't my style. But she was very young and I thought she might mature and I for my part, might liven up a little.'

He drained what remained of his coffee. 'She never did stop wanting to party every night and some of her friends were very tiresome. She soon dropped any pretence of an interest in the business. But she could be very sweet – and fun. I thought our marriage was as successful as most, but I was always conscious that it wasn't deepening at all. We seemed to be playing out an agreeable, affectionate scene day by day, but with no depth. We went on like that for two years and I thought, this is it – this is married love.'

Mark paused, looking past Claudia to the window. 'Last autumn I conceived my crazy plan of buying a house up here and, maybe, relocating the business in the north-east. We'd had a couple of good holidays in the Borders and Isabel was always more relaxed here – less driven – away from all the rackety influences.

'A friend sent me particulars of Brackenfield. It was really too big and it was run down, but it was reasonable. I loved it on sight – particularly the setting – but it was obvious that Isabel hated it, so I put it out of my mind. The idea would probably have been too expensive, anyway.

'It was a bad time for business. Boats were not people's first priority. We had only one on the stocks that autumn. It was for a man who lived in Honfleur. You know, the old port in Normandy where so many Brits have settled?

'He wasn't an experienced sailor and, when the boat was ready, I said I'd sail it over with him and show him the ropes. This was a week after the Brackenfield trip. I left my manager, Paul Jessup, in charge of the yard. He'd only worked for me for a few months but I'd found him pretty reliable and Isabel and I had become quite friendly with him and Eve, his wife.'

He stopped and a shudder ran over him. Claudia went over to him and took him in her arms.

He said dully, 'We sailed early on the Friday morning and it was evening before we had docked and completed the formalities. I was to spend the night with my client and take the Le Havre ferry home the next day. Very early on the Saturday morning the police arrived to tell me that Isabel had been killed in a car crash the previous night.

'I was completely stunned – but I was puzzled, too. Isabel hadn't planned to go out that night; in fact, she disliked night driving. I phoned Paul

Jessup a couple of times to get more details, but I couldn't reach him. It wasn't until I was back in England that I discovered that Paul had been driving the car and he was dead, too.

'At first I thought there was some innocent explanation. Perhaps Isabel had visited Paul and Eve and he was driving her home. Or that she had asked him to drive her somewhere—'

'It could have been something like that,' Claudia ventured.

Mark smiled bleakly. 'They had left a restaurant ten minutes earlier. Paul was over the limit.'

'Even so—'

'They were booked into a motel. Paul had told his wife that *he* was taking the boat to Honfleur.

'The local papers wouldn't leave it alone – Isabel's family were well known in the community. Then a couple of the national tabloids got on to it. It was the "betrayal" angle they particularly enjoyed – the "husband's best friend" scenario. Not strictly true, but I had given Paul a good salary and responsibility when he had only mediocre qualifications. But it was worse for Eve – she had two small children—'

Claudia said quietly, 'Mark, I'm no Isabel and Peter is not Paul.'

'It wasn't an experience to sustain a trusting nature. In some way it inhibited natural grieving. Humiliation and a stupid macho pride got in the way.'

'It must have been horrible for you,' Claudia said. 'But, if life hadn't come to that abrupt stop, it could have remained a trivial one-off fling. It was dishonourable, but it wasn't intended to be what the curtain came down on. It wasn't supposed to write off what you and Isabel had together, or what Paul had with his family until then.'

Mark took hold of her hand. 'You're right. I was just starting to work that out for myself when you arrived. I saw you with Peter and I thought it was the same situation all over again.'

'Oh, no, Mark!'

'I know that now.' He pulled her gently to him. 'Bear with me, Claudia. I know I'm a difficult bastard, but already you mean so much to me.'

She was at a loss for words, but none were needed. Half-sitting on the table he pulled her between his thighs. His arms tightened about her, his hands moving restlessly over her body, each caress arousing her more. His mouth met hers with desperate passion and, in a moment, she was returning his kisses with a fervour to match his own. They clung together in ecstasy, Mark's lips hot on her mouth and throat.

'Mark, oh, Mark!' Claudia's muffled cry was a mixture of longing and alarm, but the throbbing urgency of Mark's body was aroused beyond caution.

'Claudia, please—'

There was a sound of footsteps crossing the hall and Peter's voice called, 'Are you there, Mark?'

Claudia jerked away from Mark while he fought for control of himself. 'Christ, that man's timing is bloody marvellous!'

Peter pushed open the kitchen door. He stopped on sight of them. 'I'm sorry...' he began.

Mark said coolly, 'What do you want, Peter?'

Peter held out a sheaf of paper. 'I – er – made some preliminary notes. I could come back—'

Mark walked over and took the papers from

Peter who continued to stand uncomfortably in the doorway, avoiding Claudia's eye.

With a superhuman effort Mark mastered his frustration and attempted to show an interest in Peter's suggestions.

'Yes, this looks good. I've instructed the house agent to take the cottages off the market until we've done some work on them. I'll get on to the roofer and the other tradesmen this afternoon. Are you going back there now?'

Peter glanced at his watch. 'I ought to fetch the kids home.'

'Oh, of course. I'll see you later, then.'

Peter looked at Claudia. She said quickly, 'I'll come with you.' She said a swift goodbye to Mark, grabbed up her jacket and followed Peter to the door.

Outside, Peter said, 'Sorry, I interrupted something, didn't I?'

'That was pretty obvious, wasn't it? The weird thing is I'm always half-glad to be interrupted.' She smiled wryly. 'I do like him – I more than like him – but I'm scared of getting in too deep. He's been through a lot and it wouldn't be easy. I really did hope that it would be straightforward next time!'

Peter turned troubled eyes on her. 'I couldn't bear you to be unhappy, Claudia.'

'Then I won't be! Come on, we'll be late for school!'

They jogged the rest of the way to the cottage where Claudia volunteered to do the school run. As she drove the short distance to the village she thought over the recent scene with Mark. Should she back off as she had from previous budding relationships? It was tempting. It was the safe uncomplicated way. And on none of the previous occasions had she been in danger of falling so spectacularly in love as she was this time. There would be no half-measures with Mark. She could give her heart and be terribly hurt, or she could run away and miss something wonderful.

She put her quandary aside as she greeted the children and strapped them into the car.

After lunch Peter returned to work, the children settled down to their naps and Claudia and Jenny got on with household chores.

At three o'clock the children were downstairs again so restless and lively that the women decided to walk them over the hill to visit their father at the old cottages.

'Perhaps it will exhaust the little horrors,' Jenny said, 'and I really feel like a walk. I haven't had the time – or the inclination – for ages.'

'Should you walk that far?' Claudia asked anxiously. 'There's no way I can carry you all home.'

'Oh, sure. We'll take it slowly.'

The children put on their anoraks – although it was sunny there was a cool breeze – and they started out. They set a gentle pace, the children dashing about, covering twice the distance, and showing no sign of flagging.

They arrived at the cottages to find Mark and Peter engaged in clearing old masonry and other debris from the rooms into the garden. Mark's forearms below the rolled-up sleeves of his checked shirt were filthy and a fine film of white plaster deckled his dark hair. He smiled at the children as they charged up, looking more carefree than Claudia would have believed possible.

'Jenny, should you have walked all this way?' Peter protested.

'I did try to dissuade her,' Claudia put in.

'Yes, she did, but I'm fine,' Jenny said. 'I enjoyed the walk and I was keen to see what was going on here.'

'Do you notice any difference?' Mark asked.

Jenny gazed at the cottages. She looked at Mark doubtfully. 'Er – there's a bit less of them.'

Mark gave a shout of laughter. 'There's appreciation of our toil, Peter! But you have to clear the decks first. I'm moving everything that isn't attached to anything else.'

'The constructive part comes later,' Peter said. 'Here's what we have in mind.'

He spread out some sheets of paper and the four adults gathered round while he demonstrated what was planned. In some of the sketches Claudia identified Peter's bold strokes, in others Mark's meticulous draughtsmanship.

'They'll be very small, of course,' Mark said. 'But, being in a national park, there are very strict regulations about extending.'

'They're going to be very attractive.' Claudia tucked a tawny windblown lock behind her ear. Mark had not addressed a word directly to her, or met her eyes, but the tension between them was tangible.

Peter started to discuss various features in detail and, after a while, Ben began to grow restless.

He clambered up on to the low wall. 'Come here, Claudie! Come and give me a piggy-back home.'

'Forget it, kid! You walk as very very far as you can – *then* I'll give you a piggy-back.' Claudia took both his hands and swung him down from the wall.

'One, two, three, go!'

Ben scampered happily after Amy. Claudia turned back to Peter. 'Highly suggestible children you've got, but we'd better catch them up.'

She and Jenny set off after the children. Ben made it three-quarters of the way home before Claudia took him on her back. At the cottage she got the children's tea while Jenny, who was looking very tired, rested on the settee. After a while Peter came in, showered, put the children to bed, then finished preparing the evening meal with Claudia.

The next morning Claudia took the children to school leaving Jenny in bed with a breakfast tray. The few sunny days were over and a grey mist hung low over the valley. This meant that Claudia was not pleased when she returned to the cottage to find Jenny downstairs fretting about some calculations that Peter had left behind.

'It can't matter that much, surely,' she said. 'He'll be back at lunchtime.'

'I know he intended to take them with him. Mark is waiting for them.' Jenny ran a hand distractedly through her tousled hair. 'I hate to ask you, Claudia, but won't you please take them to him?'

Claudia didn't relish the idea of the long walk through wet grass and chill mist and she didn't like to leave Jenny alone looking so upset. However her irrational distress over the forgotten notes couldn't help her condition.

'All right, I'll go,' she said. 'But, please, go back to bed, Jenny. I'll see to things here as soon as I get back.'

Jenny promised meekly and Claudia buttoned up her jacket, tied a silk square over her hair and folded the papers into her pocket. It was cold leaving the cottage, but she soon became warm as she hurried up the hill. When she arrived at the cottages they seemed at first to be deserted, but, when she entered one of the tiny living-rooms, she found Peter squatting on his heels patiently scraping away loose plaster.

He looked concerned when he saw her. 'Is anything wrong?'

'No. It's only that you forgot to take these specifications. Jenny thought that you might need them.'

He straightened up and took the notes from her. 'Thanks. They could have waited till lunchtime. You needn't have walked all this way.'

'That's what I thought, but Jenny seemed to be in a bit of a state over them, so it seemed best to go along with her.'

'Yes, it is.' He pushed the notes into his jeans' pocket and wiped his dusty hands on a rag. 'I've been so worried about her. I do love her, you know, Claudia.'

'I know you do, Peter.'

'When she was first ill – capable, reliable, Jenny – it just shattered me. I realized that if anything happened to her my whole world would fall apart.'

'Nothing is going to happen to her.'

'But I was unfair to her for so long. For *years*. Oh, I always loved her, but you, Claudia, had my dreams.'

Claudia smiled wryly. 'It was the same with me. Time we grew up, wouldn't you say?'

He took both her hands in his, holding them against his chest. 'Do you know what I think our problem was? We never said goodbye.' He pulled her gently towards him and kissed her, with affection and a trace of sadness, but without passion. Then he drew back. 'That was the full-stop we never had time for.'

They saw Mark at the same moment. He was standing outside in the little garden watching them through the window, his eyes dark with distaste. In icy tones, he said, 'You may be interested to know that Jenny is ill. She just phoned the house. She thinks she should go to hospital.'

Nine

Neither Claudia or Peter felt a flicker of guilt. Their action had been so innocent that they felt only concern for Jenny.

Claudia exclaimed, 'I knew I shouldn't have left her!'

'There's no time for remorse now,' Mark snapped. 'I've got the car outside the house, it will be quicker to drive down.'

The three of them hurried up the hill towards Brackenfield, Peter plying Mark with questions. Mark's car was standing at the front door and they scrambled into it. Mark drove swiftly down the drive and along the track to the cottage.

By now Claudia was aware that he was in a furious temper and that he had, once again, misinterpreted what he had seen, but she was too concerned with Jenny's condition to dwell on it.

Peter burst into the cottage with Claudia at his heels. Jenny was sitting upright on a kitchen chair, her face chalk-white. Peter ran to her and put his arms around her. 'Darling, what is it?'

'I wasn't doing anything strenuous, honestly,' Jenny said. 'I was only washing the breakfast dishes when I had a very bad pain. O-oh—' Her face tightened.

Claudia knelt beside her. 'You promised you'd go back to bed,' she scolded, close to tears.

Peter kissed Jenny's forehead. 'Is the case packed?' At her nod, 'Come on, sweetheart, we'll get you to hospital.'

Jenny clutched Claudia's arm. 'Will you come, Claudia?'

'Of course, I will. But what about Amy and Ben?'

Mark was still at the door. 'Don't worry about the children. I'll take care of them.'

'Would you, Mark?' Jenny's face lightened. 'I should like Claudia with me.'

'I'll take my car and follow you,' Claudia said. 'Then I can get back here if Peter wants to stay.'

Peter helped Jenny to her feet and supported her to the door while Claudia collected the ready-packed overnight bag.

As Mark stood aside for them to pass, Claudia gave him the key to the cottage. 'The children get out of playschool at twelve-thirty. You know where it is?' He nodded curtly. 'Amy will be able to tell you where to find something for their lunch. Then they usually have a rest.' Her eyes met his briefly. 'You'll – you'll reassure them? Don't let them get frightened about Jenny.'

'Don't worry about them.'

Claudia hurried after Peter and Jenny. Peter had settled Jenny in his car. Claudia put the bag on to their back seat and got into her own car as Peter headed slowly for the gates. In fifteen minutes they had reached the small cottage hospital. Peter parked near the entrance and Claudia pulled in beside him. He helped Jenny from the car while Claudia took the bag and they all went into the entrance hall and up to the reception desk.

In a very few minutes the staff, who combined efficiency with warmth, had Jenny tucked into bed awaiting a doctor's attention.

Turned out into the waiting area, Peter paced distractedly. 'Oh, God, Claudia – if anything should go wrong!'

'Try not to worry, Peter, she's in the right place now. They'll do all they can.'

It was easily said, but for the next hour they waited on tenterhooks until the doctor arrived to tell them that Jenny was comfortable and they had stabilized her condition, but would like to keep her under observation for a couple of days.

Peter and Claudia went in to see her, finding her drifting off into a sedated sleep in the bright little ward. After fifteen minutes Claudia left to return to the cottage and take over the children. Peter intended to stay with Jenny for a time.

In the car Claudia relaxed her shoulders for what felt like the first time that day, relieved that her not being at hand when the emergency occurred had had no serious effect on Jenny.

Mark was another concern, but one she didn't intend to worry about at present. He had obviously misunderstood what had passed between her and Peter and he probably wouldn't believe her denial, but she felt armoured by their innocence. She had a fleeting qualm about the security of the Liddells' cottage, but she couldn't believe that Mark would change his mind over it.

In a short time the gates of Brackenfield came into view. Claudia parked near the cottage, switched off the engine and drew a deep breath.

The cottage appeared to be deserted. Then she heard voices and, going to the kitchen window, saw

Mark, Ben and Amy tossing a ball between them in the back garden, all three looking quite at ease with each other.

In a moment, Amy spotted Claudia and rushed into the house. 'Hello, Claudia! Mark is playing a game with us. We had spaghetti and bananas for our dinner.'

Claudia hugged her. 'Not at the same time, I hope.'

Amy laughed. 'No! Bananas were pudding.'

Mark had followed her in, gently bouncing the ball off Ben's head. 'Was that OK?'

'The menu? Sounds fine to me. Did you have any problems?'

'No, none at all. How is Jenny?'

Claudia glanced at the children, although they seemed to have forgotten their parents in the novelty of the situation. 'Wash your hands now, children.'

As they jostled at the sink, she led the way into the living-room. 'She's comfortable – she was asleep when I left. They're fairly sure the baby will be all right.'

'Thank God for that.'

Ben and Amy, thoroughly damp, pushed in to join them. 'Claudia, where is Mummy?' Amy asked.

'Mummy has to stay at the hospital for a little while,' Claudia told her. 'Just for a few days to have a rest.'

Amy's mouth dropped. 'Who will look after us?'

'Why, I will, darling. And Daddy will be here.'

'And Uncle Mark!' Ben shouted, hanging from Mark's hand.

'Daddy will be home this evening,' Claudia reassured them. 'He'll come up to see you before you go to sleep. Which reminds me – it's time for your nap now.'

There were loud protests and Ben would not be mollified until Mark, too, came up to settle them into bed.

Coming downstairs, Claudia said, 'I'm going to make myself a sandwich, I missed lunch. How about you?'

'No, thanks. I ate with the children.'

Claudia went out to the kitchen where she started the coffee and inspected the fridge hopefully.

Mark watched her from the doorway. 'They're great kids.'

'Yes, aren't they?'

'Isn't Peter spending the night at the hospital?'

'No. Jenny thought the children would be less upset if he was here. After all, they've only known me for a short time.'

Mark came further into the kitchen. His back half-turned from her, he said, 'That's very convenient for you.'

Claudia, who had been slicing bread, suddenly lost her appetite. 'What did you say?'

'I said that it was convenient for you that Jenny was so trusting.'

Claudia took a deep breath, but her voice, when it emerged, was shaking. 'I realize your personal experience has influenced you. I'm making every allowance for that. But if you're suggesting that Peter or I would abuse Jenny's absence – in her home – and with the children here—' She faltered into silence, her face stricken.

'My personal experience has nothing to do with this. *I saw you, Claudia!*'

Claudia gave up any thought of lunch, pushing the plate away and wiping her hands on a towel. 'It wasn't like that. I told you – whatever there was between Peter and me is over.'

'Yet you fall into each other's arms at every opportunity.'

'I wouldn't expect you to understand but – we were saying goodbye.'

'So you did intend to leave?'

'No, I wasn't going away.'

'But you *were* saying goodbye?'

Her shoulders sagged. 'We were saying goodbye to all the foolish years we wasted yearning after each other. Peter said we had never put a full-stop to them – and so, we did. Oh, I don't know why I'm even trying to explain to you!'

He turned to look at her fully. Her eyes pleaded with him. His face a tightly controlled mask, he said, 'But it's your job to keep me on a string, isn't it? A little tug on the line now and again when it looks as though I'm getting away? Isn't that what you were brought in for?'

'I didn't even know you existed when I came here.' She swallowed. 'Mark, please, whatever you think of me – or of Peter – don't change your mind over the cottage. It wouldn't be fair to Jenny and the children.'

'What do you take me for? As far as I'm concerned, Peter could sleep on the streets, but Jenny has enough to put up with as it is. As for you, I'd be grateful if you'd stay out of my way for the rest of your time here!'

He turned quickly and left the room and Claudia sank into a chair, her legs shaking. She couldn't blame Mark for what he thought of her and Peter, but his low opinion hurt terrribly. At least the Liddells' home was safe. He had given his word and she was sure he would keep it. And, as he had requested, she would stay out of the way, because if she had to see him she thought her heart would break.

After a while she got up and made some coffee. The children would be downstairs soon and it was up to her to see that they were untroubled by Jenny's absence.

When she had drunk her coffee, she tidied the room and made plans for dinner. When the children came down she read to them and organized games until their teatime. By early evening they were becoming tearful and querulous and she was relieved to hear Peter arriving home.

She was relieved, too, to see his cheerful expression as he looked into the kitchen.

'Hi! I didn't expect you for a bit. How is Jenny?'

'She says she feels very well, and they're sure everything is going to be all right.'

'That's great, Peter!'

He grinned at her dishevelled hair. 'How was everything here? Are you at the end of your tether?'

'Not at all – bags of tether left. The children have been very good. They're just starting to get a little fractious now.'

'I'll go and talk to them. How did Mark manage?'

'Extremely well. He seems to have been a great hit.'

Peter paused. The noise from the living-room rose alarmingly. 'Did he say anything about this morning – at the cottage? I thought he seemed rather—'

'Yes, he did and he was. I tried to set him straight, but – oh, well, it doesn't matter. It's still OK about the cottage. He won't change his mind over that.'

'That's all right, then.' Peter sighed with relief. 'I'll go and see the kids. Pour us some drinks, Claudia, it's been quite a day.'

He went to the children who, after briefly resorting to babyhood with tears and cuddles, returned to their usual cheerful selves. When they had been bathed and tucked up in bed, Peter and Claudia relaxed with a quiet drink before dinner. Later in the evening, Peter telephoned the hospital to ascertain that all was well with Jenny. Then he and Claudia talked in a desultory fashion for a while before turning in for an early night.

The next morning Peter left early for work and Claudia took the children to school. By 10.30 she had cleaned up and done some washing and was sitting down with a cup of coffee when Peter came in.

He poured himself some coffee. 'I'm going over to the hospital for an hour. Any messages for Jenny?'

'Just give her my love and tell her everything is fine here.' She hesitated. 'Was Mark all right with you?'

'Mark has gone.'

'What?'

'He must have left sometime yesterday. The house is locked up and the car has gone.'

'What about the work on the cottages?'

'That's not affected. The roofers are already on the site. The foreman said that Mark had told him on the phone to take his orders from me – I know how the work is to progress.'

Claudia was silent. Then she said, 'Has he gone away before?'

'Not without letting me know. I shall miss him on the job. I'd got to like him in the last few days. When you told me about his wife – that explained a lot.'

'Yes, it does,' Claudia agreed. But she had only told Peter that Mark's wife had been killed. The rest of the painful story, that explained so much more, she was sure he wouldn't want discussed.

She packed some of Jenny's favourite biscuits, picked a bunch of spring flowers from the garden and sent Peter on his way.

From that time on, life was different at Brackenfield. Claudia could concentrate on running the house and caring for the children without Mark's disturbing presence. It was peaceful, but there was an emptiness in knowing that she would not meet him as she walked the hillside and feel that leap of excitement. He phoned Peter to discuss work on the cottages. He enquired about Jenny, but he never mentioned Claudia. At the end of five days, Jenny left hospital looking fully restored.

After that, Claudia split her time between Brackenfield and Durham. She fulfilled her outstanding commissions, but she sought no new projects and neglected the networking that had previously brought in new work and contracts. She had little social life. Her apartment, once a source of such pleasure and pride, looked unloved.

In late May Jenny went into early labour and, with a minimum of fuss, produced a baby girl. After a hectic week at the cottage following Jenny's return from hospital, Claudia returned permanently to Durham. Externally the two old cottages were now near completion and Peter had little to do. During this time Mark had returned briefly to Brackenfield on a couple of occasions, but, whether by accident or design his visits did not coincide with Claudia's.

In June Claudia spent a week in Rome, an attempt to recapture her old zest which left her feeling more wretched than before. The day after she returned, Jenny telephoned to ask her to stand as godmother to baby Elizabeth.

'You weren't around when the other two were "done",' Jenny explained when Claudia had expressed her delight, 'and we're scraping the barrel now.'

'Thank you, Jenny. You really know how to make a person feel wanted!'

'I was only joking. You were always our first choice, but we saw so little of you then. Anyway, that's great, Peter will be so pleased. Karen is going to be the other one. You remember Karen from playgroup?'

'Of course. Who is to be godfather?'

'You won't believe it, but it's going to be Mark! I wouldn't have asked him, but I was talking about the christening when he was there – about how we had used up all our male friends on Amy and Ben – and he offered. Said he would be honoured.'

There was a brief pause. Then Claudia said, 'Does he know that I'm to be a godmother?'

'Yes, he does. At least, he knew I was going to ask you. What's the matter, Claudia? Peter said you'd had some sort of showdown with Mark on the morning I went into hospital and that's why he had cleared off—' Jenny waited. Claudia made no response and she continued in, what was for her, an unusually sharp voice. 'Frankly, I think you're being unreasonable. Whatever went wrong between you two, I'm sure he has forgotten about it and I think you should do the same.'

He won't have forgotten, Claudia thought. He despises me because he thinks I tried to steal your husband while you were bearing his child. There was no way Jenny could ever be told the reason for their antagonism.

She said, 'Do you think he's suitable?'

'We think he's perfect. I know we all got off on the wrong foot, but he's been very considerate and generous for the last few months. He's flexible over Peter's hours and he pays him a ridiculously large wage. Perhaps it's our fault for complaining so bitterly about him to you at the start, but, believe me, he's completely changed.'

Again Claudia was silent and, after a moment, Jenny said, 'If it's a problem for you, I'll put him off, Claudia. Obviously we must have you.'

'Don't be silly! There's no problem at all.' Claudia moved on to safer ground. 'How are the cottages coming along?'

'They're almost finished. They look great.'

'What will Peter do now?'

'Goodness knows. He spends most of his time helping me as it is.'

They chatted a little longer and Jenny gave Claudia the date and time of the christening.

For the next three weeks Claudia's emotions were in turmoil. She looked forward to the baptism and her role in it – but she viewed seeing Mark again with a mixture of dread and longing. How should she react to him? How would he behave towards her? Perhaps, back with his old life, he had forgotten her, as Jenny had suggested.

The weather was unusually warm and she tossed restlessly on her bed through the night, conjuring up possible scenarios.

She strove to fill her days, throwing herself into her work as she hadn't done since pre-Mark times. The evenings she spent sewing outfits for the children, a dainty lawn dress for the baby, one in bright cotton for Amy, sturdy dungarees for Ben.

At last the day arrived, as warm and sunny as the previous two weeks. After much indecision and rehearsal, Claudia had decided to wear an elegant Italian suit in cream raw silk which set off her tawny hair and lightly tanned skin. Matched with black pumps and bag it went some way to giving her the confidence she needed.

She loaded the car with the children's clothes and her gift for the baby. The countryside looked beautiful and normally she would have enjoyed the drive on the quiet Sunday roads, but apprehension seized her, bringing out fine perspiration on her body and drying her throat. As she passed Otterburn she felt so sick with nerves that it was as much as she could do not to turn around and go back.

There was no church at Marling, so the ceremony was to be held at the tiny church in the next village. Guests, however, were to rendezvous first at the Liddells' home. Claudia had timed her journey in order not to arrive ahead of the others and, as she turned between the gates of Bracken-field, she met a group of young women that she recognized as playgroup mothers.

Claudia waved. She drove slowly along the track to the parking place, now home to half-a-dozen cars, including Mark's. She sat for a moment trying to control her rising panic. When the young women drew abreast, Claudia got out with her packages and tagged on at the back of the group.

The cottage appeared crowded. Claudia's swift, flurried glance took in Jenny attempting to subdue Ben's hair and Karen, the playgroup head, buttoning the back of Amy's dress. Two other women were putting the finishing touches to the buffet table. Baby Elizabeth, in a froth of lace, lay in a carrycot on the settee.

Jenny spotted Claudia and rushed to hug her, Ben and Amy following. Claudia greeted everyone and handed over the gifts.

'Peter, Claudia is here!' Jenny called and Peter came through from the dining-room with another man. Behind them, looking over their heads, was Mark.

Claudia's reaction was even stronger than she had feared – a great enveloping wave of emotion that left her knees weak. Then she was crushed in Peter's embrace. 'Claudia, you look fantastic!'

He released her and introduced the young man who turned out to be Karen's husband. 'And, of course, you remember Mark?'

Something unfathomable flickered in Mark's eyes. 'Don't be ridiculous, Peter.' He took Claudia's hand. 'So – we are to play mother and father?'

Claudia's cheeks flamed as she endeavoured to turn the handclasp into a shake. 'How are you, Mark?'

'I'm well. And you? You look – radiant.'

'I'm fine. Very busy. I've just got back from Rome.' It sounded dashing and drew a veil over three weeks of evenings spent sewing baby clothes.

Beside them Jenny was displaying the garments to the admiring guests. 'Aren't they beautiful? Look at the hand-sewing, it's so delicate.'

'And so time-consuming,' Mark drawled quietly.

Claudia's irritation was masked by Jenny's sudden awareness of the time and a scramble to get her guests organized to leave for the church.

'We invited Mrs Cunningham,' she said, hoisting Elizabeth's carrycot on to her hip, 'but she didn't feel up to it. She sent a lovely little string of cultured pearls.'

'I fear Mrs Cunningham was a hard act to follow,' Mark said.

'Oh, Mark, you've been terribly generous!' Jenny protested. Behind his back she mouthed at Claudia, 'Big cheque!'

Amy took Mark's and Claudia's hand, skipping between them to the car, while Claudia gritted her teeth at the domesticity of the scene. They were mercifully separated at the cars where Claudia loaded two of the playgroup mums in with Amy.

The journey took only ten minutes through quiet lanes before they reached the village and its small stone church. Claudia and Amy slipped into a pew behind Peter and Jenny with the baby. A moment later, Mark edged in beside them.

When they were called to the font, Jenny passed Elizabeth to Claudia and parents and godparents circled the ancient bowl. Claudia looked down at the baby's sleeping face as she made her solemn promises. Handed over to the priest, Elizabeth woke only for a brief startled yelp as the water touched her forehead, then returned to sleep. At the end of the service everyone filed out into brilliant sunshine, thanking the priest who waited at the door.

'She was so good!' Claudia said, still carrying the baby.

'I fed her to bursting point,' Jenny explained. 'Now it's our turn and I, for one, am starving. How long can you stay, Claudia?'

Claudia glanced at her watch. 'I should get off by five.'

Mark swung Ben up on to his shoulders. 'Still on the wing?'

'Is Claudia a bird?' Ben shouted.

'Superwoman, I think, Ben.' He led the way down the churchyard path to the cars. Over his shoulder he said to Claudia, 'Why don't you have a look at the cottages while you're here? The transformation is unbelievable.'

'Jenny said they were very attractive.' Claudia handed the baby to Peter who secured the carrycot in the back of his car. 'Perhaps – if there is time.'

Mark looked at her half-mockingly. 'You'll be quite safe. No broken glass.'

She smiled uncertainly as she put Amy in the car, looking round for her other passengers who, fortunately, at that moment came hurrying up.

The cars moved back towards Brackenfield and, as she kept her position, Claudia reflected on Mark's manner towards her. It would seem that he had called a truce, at least in public. It was hard to believe that he had forgotten his bitter words at their last meeting. But, once back at the cottage, the activity put it out of her mind. Jenny was in high spirits and a party atmosphere soon built up as food and drink circulated, conversation grew animated and the children ran about excitedly among the guests.

As she had a long drive ahead of her, Claudia confined herself to a single glass of wine and took over as hostess, ferrying refills to the guests and empty dishes to the kitchen while Jenny relaxed. On one journey she turned from the sink to find Mark behind her, his hands full of plates.

'Where do you want these?'

'Oh, any vacant spot you can find. I'll get to them in a minute.'

He cleared a space on the kitchen table. 'Why don't you relax? Everyone in there is perfectly happy.'

Claudia pushed back a strand of hair. 'Yes, it's going well, isn't it? It's wonderful to see Jenny looking so well and happy.'

'I believe you really mean that.'

'Of course, I mean it.'

He came closer to her so that it was difficult for her to move in the enclosed space. 'Claudia, I owe you a tremendous apology—'

She squirmed uncomfortably in an effort to get back to the rest of the company. 'Please – don't go on. I doesn't matter.'

'It matters to me – more than I can say. Will you come for a walk – just for a few minutes? There are some things I must straighten out with you.'

'I can't.' She glanced desperately towards the half-open door of the living-room and the babble of talk and laughter, praying for rescue. 'I must clear up in here—'

'Claudia.' He took both her hands in his. 'You don't have to organize things. That isn't why Jenny invited you. People can manage without you – except me.'

There was no mistaking the naked longing on his

face and she dropped her eyes before it. 'Mark, I can't go through this again.'

'What are you so afraid to confront in yourself? I know you care for me.'

She half-swayed towards him as Ben erupted into the kitchen. 'More icecream, Claudie!'

'Ben – out!' Mark said firmly, his arms around Claudia. Ben climbed on to a chair to better view the interesting situation.

Mark laughed. 'We're beaten,' he said to Claudia. 'Let's slip out the back way.' As she hesitated, 'I need your advice.'

They went out by the back door and turned up the hill. 'I can't stay long—' Claudia began.

'Don't!' Mark said in the same tone he had used to Ben. 'Don't say that again.'

They walked on for a few yards. 'What did you want advice about?' Claudia asked meekly.

'What? Well, we could talk about the cottages. They're a bit small for dwellings and we're not permitted to extend them, so I thought of renting them for holiday use.'

'I should think they would be very suitable. The country is beautiful and it's central for touring Northumberland and the Border country. But don't you need a cash sale to keep up Brackenfield?'

'I sold my house in Welsea. It was much smaller than Brackenfield, but the prices around there are ridiculous so the cash problem is solved.'

'Does that mean—?' Claudia hesitated. 'Will you settle here permanently?'

They had reached Brackenfield now. The house looked warm and gracious in the afternoon sunshine.

'I don't know. It's much too big for one. I've bought a small marina flat in Welsea, so I can still commute.'

They crested the hill and dropped down on the other side. Immediately below them Claudia saw the restored cottages, newly roofed and freshly painted with sturdy walls round the little gardens.

'Oh, they're charming! I can't believe it!'

'Jenny is going to prepare and illustrate a brochure. Peter's work is finished now, so he'll be off the payroll.'

They had started down the hill towards the cottages, but at Mark's words, Claudia stopped abruptly and turned to him, her heart lurching. Were they back to the old man-or-monster Mark? Back to the situation that had put her heart on this roller-coaster?

He saw the shock on her face. 'Don't look like that. I'm sure you agree that it's time Peter was kicked out of the nest? He has the abilities for much better things. I'll pay his wages until he can find something more worthy of him, but I'll expect him to look damned hard. They can keep the cottage rent-free if Jenny will manage the holiday bookings. That will give her an interest outside the family.'

Claudia smiled her relief. 'And you accuse me of running other people's lives! Have you talked to them about this?'

'I've talked to Jenny. She's one hundred per cent behind the idea. She's very keen for Peter to get back to painting and teaching.'

They had reached the cottages and Mark opened the nearer gate for Claudia. 'Will you come into my parlour? They're already decorated – Jenny advised on that – but I thought you might have some ideas on furnishings.'

Claudia went into the living-room. It had been attractively decorated in a way that made the most of the limited space.

'It's delightful. What a transformation!'

'The workmen were excellent and Peter and Jenny came up with some brilliant ideas.'

Claudia inspected the compact and ingenious kitchen, then climbed the open staircase to see the two pretty bedrooms and the tiny shower-room.

'I'm very impressed. You don't need me.' She shuddered at the wistful note that crept into her voice.

'Putting that to one side – you could advise on the furnishings.'

She walked to the window and looked out at the valley, shining emerald and gold in the sun. 'Jenny could do that.'

'I'd like you to have some part in it.'

'I'm sorry. I don't think I can spare the time.'

He flinched at the rebuff in her words and Claudia said quickly, 'I'm very grateful to you for being so generous to Jenny and Peter.'

'I misjudged Peter. It was plain that he had been crazy about you. That was easy for me to understand. But I should have seen how much he loved Jenny.

'Weeks later he gave me the measurements that you had brought to him that morning. You remember – the morning that Jenny was taken ill?' At her pained nod he went on, 'He had forgotten all about them and found them in a pocket. He told me that you had only arrived with them moments before I got there and he had filled those moments telling you how much he loved Jenny. He told me about the "goodbye" kiss.'

Claudia said bleakly, 'I was such an idiot – all those wasted years.'

'I have a theory about that.' He was so close to her now that she felt his warm breath on her cheek. 'I think you kept that love alive because you were afraid of what might take its place. I know your love for Peter was very real – but you could deal with it. If it was over it could have left you open to something more powerful, more painful—'

He put his hands on her shoulders and turned her to face him. 'Don't make me beg, Claudia, it's not my style.'

She made no answer and he raised her chin and kissed her softly on the mouth. Desperately, she whispered, 'Mark, I'm afraid—'

'Of what, Claudia? I know you care.'

She dropped her face to his shoulder. 'It's like you said – I'm afraid that I would care too much.'

'You couldn't. You couldn't care too much. That was something else I meant to ask you. A matter of a vacancy – and a tenant.'

She looked around blankly. 'A vacancy? For the cottage?'

'No. In my heart. A great, aching, black hole of a vacancy that's waiting for a tenant. Claudia, my love, please don't take wing again.'

She went into his arms, a response as instinctive as finding her way home and as exciting as an electrical storm. Her body pressed to his as her mouth sought deeper kisses. Then, breaking away just for a moment, she murmured against his ear, 'Never again. Claudia is ready to alight!'